# ENEMY OF MAGIC

## DRAGON'S GIFT THE PROTECTOR BOOK 4

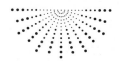

## LINSEY HALL

*To Kathryn, who is wonderful.*

# CHAPTER ONE

Magic flowed around me as I stood at a table in my trove, pruning a desert rose. I snipped off a branch, and I swore I could feel the gratitude of the plant.

"My new magic is nuts," I muttered.

*Okay, crazy lady.* Talking to myself wasn't my thing, but oddly, I felt like I had company.

*Ha.* More like an imaginary friend.

Maybe I was just growing closer with my Life magic, the extent of which I still didn't understand.

A fluttering sounded from behind me. I turned. The explosion of greenery sat still and calm—flowers, fruit, and trees all resting quietly. Not a leaf or petal moved.

Weird. I'd sworn I'd heard something.

Nah, I was crazy.

I shrugged and turned back to the desert rose, then snipped an errant branch, letting my magic feel the plant's energy.

It'd been two days since I'd used my new magic against Drakon to destroy his mortal body and released the smoky dragon that was his true form. I hadn't managed to figure out exactly how I'd done it, but I'd need to if I wanted to stand a chance against him.

Another fluttering sounded, this time from my right. I whirled to find it, but saw nothing. Just one banana leaf quivering in a nonexistent breeze.

I was clearly going nuts. It was impossible for anyone but me and my *deirfiúr* to enter my trove. If it were Cass or Del, they would call out to me. Had to be nothing.

I focused on the desert rose, enjoying the few stolen minutes caring for my garden. These were the only minutes I'd get.

I'd woken early to steal this time, but soon, I'd need to meet Cass and Del to start our work. Ares, too. We were staring down the barrel of another long day hunting Drakon and dragons.

The back of my neck prickled, the hair standing on end.

*I was being watched.*

I knew it like I knew my own name. I was *not* crazy. Despite my certainty that no one else could enter my trove, something was up. I spun around, searching. A flash of movement to the left caught my eye and I whirled.

It was gone.

But I wasn't imagining things. I sprinted toward it, dodging a potted palm and jumping over a bag of soil. I skidded as I turned right, spying another flash of movement. Something small. Something flying.

Had a bird gotten in here? Occasionally, I opened the skylights for fresh air, but with the chaos of the last few weeks, I hadn't had a chance.

I hurried toward the bird, darting around tables and benches covered with plants. A flare of red, then green, drew me toward the middle of my trove.

"Come out, little bird!" I called.

There was a strange hissing noise. Not birdlike. I shivered, but forced myself forward.

As I turned the corner, moving around a bench that held several tall palms, I caught sight of it.

My mind turned to static like an old TV.

That was no bird.

That was a *dragon.*

My breath whooshed out of my lungs. *Holy fates.*

The little dragon was only the size of a terrier. Its wings were a beautiful shining red and its body covered in glittering green scales. The belly was an opalescent white, speckled with black dots. Gleaming black eyes peered intelligently at me as the dragon fluttered its wings to hover in midair.

Then it disappeared.

*Shit!*

Where had it gone? I hurried forward, desperately searching for the dragon.

"Come back!" It had been real, hadn't it?

Across the room, the huge leaves of a banana plant rustled. I raced toward it, catching sight of the little dragon as it darted around the leaves.

There was no way I was making this up, right? But where the heck had he come from?

By the time I reached the banana plant, the dragon was gone. My gaze caught on one of the pots that held my dragon fruit plant. At the base of the plant's thick green stalk were the remains of a dragon fruit. The white flesh was gone, leaving only the red and green peel.

I bent down and picked it up, my brow wrinkling as I inspected the shell.

What the heck? I took better care of my plants than this—and this wasn't how a dragon fruit looked when it fell off the stalk and rotted.

This was the same plant that I had touched a few days ago. My magic had sparked then, reacting to the plant. *Oh, boy.*

I looked up and around, searching for the dragon. But he was nowhere to be found. I looked for several more minutes, listening intently, but couldn't find him.

Mind whirring, I hurried for the exit of my trove. I needed backup on this. A second set of eyes that would confirm I wasn't crazy and inventing the little dragon.

As carefully as I could, I slipped out the door, determined not the let the dragon escape. I took the stairs two at a time, hurtling out into my apartment and racing through to the main exit. I sprinted down the stairs and out the door, turning right toward Potions & Pastilles. I was supposed to meet everyone there at seven thirty, and it was nearly that time.

The morning was cool and quiet as I hurried down the street. Across the road, newly placed guards lurked in the shadows of the trees in the park.

With Drakon on the hunt, Ares, Aidan, and Roarke had insisted on installing guards around our property. I was no idiot, so I'd quickly agreed it was a good idea. The vampires, demons, and members of Aidan's staff blended with the shadows, waiting to ambush any of Drakon's men, but they hadn't had a chance yet.

For whatever reason, Drakon hadn't made his move on us. And we weren't ready to act as bait—we needed more information and a better plan first. And we had neither.

I pushed open the doors to P & P, and the warmth inside rushed over me, bringing with it the scent of coffee and baked goods.

Besides Connor, who was busy behind the counter, only Cass and Del were within. They sat in our favorite chairs, sipping from white mugs. Ares wasn't here yet, but he'd planned to meet us. He'd spent the last two days hunting for information in the Vampire realm. They had their own seers and scholars who might know something. Though dragons were from our world and not theirs, *everyone* was interested in dragons.

I hurried over, panting.

"Whoa, you okay?" Cass asked.

"See a ghost?" Del asked.

"I don't know." My heart thundered in my ears. Words tumbled from my lips. "A dragon. I think I saw a dragon."

Cass leaned forward, brow creased. "What do you mean?"

"There's a little dragon in my trove. Not like the big ones we're searching for. But a little one. Maybe made of magic, like your dragonet friends." Cass had four magical dragon buddies who occasionally showed up when she was in a pickle. They weren't the enormous flesh-and-blood dragons of old that had disappeared long ago, but rather little creatures born of magic and myth.

"Did you just see it now?" Del asked.

"Yes." I nodded frantically. "I don't know how it appeared in my trove, but it's there now. You need to come look at it. You have to tell me I'm not crazy. This is important."

"You're not crazy." Del stood. "And you're right. It's important."

"Good." Relief flowed through me.

Cass stood as well, and I turned toward the door. The little dragon appeared out of the air, fluttering in the middle of the cafe.

"Holy crap." Del stumbled backward. "That's a dragon."

"Yep." Cass's eyes were wide as saucers. "He looks more solid than my dragonets."

"Yeah." I nodded. Hers were made of the elements—flame, water, smoke, and stone. This guy looked real almost.

I held out a hand, and he fluttered toward me. Up close, I could see that he was semi-transparent, but not quite like Cass's dragonets. His red, green, and white scales shimmered in the light. He sniffed my hand, then backed up, inquisitive eyes meeting mine.

"What in the world?" Connor hurried over, stopping a few feet away.

The dragon looked at him, then back at me.

"Connor?" I said. "Could you bring out some food? A variety. Oh, and a dragon fruit if you have it."

"On it." Connor hurried away, glancing back over his shoulder at the little dragon.

"This is crazy," Del said.

The dragon fluttered over to a chair and perched on the back. I sat in the chair next to him.

"What are you?" I asked.

The dragon purred. Like a cat. I reached for him, and he sniffed my fingers again, then let me pet him. My heart thundered as I carefully stroked his smooth head. Though he was mildly transparent, he was also solid to the touch. Magic sparked from him, like bubbles popping against my skin.

"Uh, this is a bit weird," Cass said. "But I really think his magic smells a heck of a lot like yours."

"Feels like it too," Del said. "Like he's your kid or something."

"Really?" I stared at the little dragon. He felt familiar. I couldn't smell or sense his magic, but maybe that was because it was like my own. I was just used to it.

"I've got an assortment," Connor called as he came over. He set a heavy tray on the coffee table and stepped back, grinning. "Not often I get to serve a dragon."

The little dragon showed no interest in the food, which looked pretty tasty to me. There were sliced apples, carrots, a cheese and potato pasty, dragon fruit, a variety of sweets, some little chunks of raw meat, along with some ham, and a bowl of water.

"Everything a dragon could possibly want." I held up a piece of apple.

He ignored it. He also ignored the carrots, pasty, ham, and the water. He didn't even want the dragon fruit, which meant that he probably hadn't eaten the one in my trove. Though he might be full, I'd think he'd at least sniff it or look vaguely tempted. But he wasn't into it.

"Maybe he doesn't eat," Cass said.

"Possibly. Especially if he's made of magic," Del said.

He gave me one last look, and poofed away.

"Where does he go when he does that?" I asked.

"Is he teleporting?" Cass asked.

"No idea." I frowned. "I hope he comes back."

"If he followed you here, I bet he will."

"Yeah." It didn't feel like a full goodbye, at least. "I know we're supposed to go hunt Drakon and the dragons today, but I'd like to go to Elesius for an hour. Just to see if my mother knows anything about this. She's my only contact who knows about my Life magic."

"I say do it," Cass said. "We need to know more about your gift. And this dragon is a big deal."

"We're headed to Dr. Garriso's anyway," Del said. "He's supposed to give us any info he has on the prophecy."

Hopefully our friend at the Museum for Magical History would recognize the line from the prophecy. *Deep in the place where the earth meets the sun and the mist meets the magma* definitely sounded like a clue to the lost dragons' location, though we couldn't be sure.

"Perfect," I said. "I'll head to Elesius for an hour, then we'll meet up and figure out what's next."

"Maybe you should wait and take Ares with you," Cass said.

I looked out the window, searching for him. He should have been here by now. "He could be delayed. I'll be fine alone."

Cass frowned. "I know. I just worry, since I can't see it for myself."

"I'm sorry. But it really will be fine." Ares could cross the barrier into Elesius because he was a Realm Walker. To get Cass and Del over would take some serious dark magic. Like the kind that had allowed Drakon's men to ambush the place. None of us were willing to use that.

"Hang on." I looked at Del. "Before we go, I wanted to ask. A couple of days ago, Ares healed you with his blood. Have you felt some kind of connection with him since then? Like an added awareness?"

"No." Del shook her head.

"So it's just me." I leaned back in my chair, unsure if I was happy or sad about that. The blood Ares had given me to heal had also given me a greater awareness of his presence and emotions. In return, the process had given him the ability to find me wherever I was.

"Sorry, friend," Del said. "Maybe it's not such a bad thing."

"Maybe not." I just hoped my feelings for him were real. I thought they were—how could I not like a guy as honorable and good as Ares?—but it was impossible to know for sure as long as we shared this blood connection.

I stood and turned toward the door. Ares appeared on the street at that moment, having transported from somewhere. Likely the Vampire Realm. I hadn't seen him in two days, and he was a sight for sore eyes. His dark hair was mussed as if he'd been running, and his clothes were slightly wrinkled. He'd been on the hunt for clues, too, utilizing every connection he had. Hopefully he'd had better luck than the rest of us.

"Good luck with Dr. Garriso." I waved goodbye to Del and Nix.

Ares met me on the sidewalk, his eyes intent on me. "How are you?"

"I've got something amazing to tell you."

"Could it wait just one moment?"

"Sure. For what?"

He leaned down and crushed his lips to mine. His body was so close that his warmth soaked into me, banishing the winter chill in the air. I wanted to press myself against the hard, muscled expanse of him. So I did, wrapping my arms around his neck and falling into the kiss. It took my breath away, until finally, Ares had to be the one who pulled back, his gaze hot on mine.

"I missed you," he said.

"I miss you, too."

"Though I'm afraid I haven't learned much. I have one lead to pursue, but nothing concrete."

Disappointment welled briefly, but it was tamped down by the memory of the dragon. "Guess what?"

"What?"

"I have a dragon." The words spilled out as I explained my new friend. "So I'm going to Elesius to ask my mother if she knows anything about this."

"You think it's related to your new magic?"

"Maybe. That's my working theory, at least."

"I'll go with you."

"All right." Truthfully, I was glad he was coming. Though I loved my home, seeing it dead and barren—because of me—was hard enough to do alone. With him at my side, it might be a bit easier to ignore the guilt. And the knowledge that if I wanted Elesius to survive, I'd have to return there to live out my days so that my Life magic could sustain the place. "Let's go."

Ares gripped my hand, his own warm and firm. "Lead the way."

As my mother had taught me, I closed my eyes and focused on Elesius, envisioning the treeless mountains and beautiful stone buildings winding up the valley ridge. A moment later, the ether pulled me in, throwing me across space as I hurtled toward my destination.

I slammed into something hard, pain flaring in my nose and chest, then bounced backward onto the ground. I landed hard on my butt, temporarily blinded by the shock. Clumsily, I scrambled upright, blinking to clear my vision.

Ares rose from the ground to stand at my side, clearly having slammed into the same thing I had. I stared at it, confusion and horror turning my chest to a wasteland.

The dome-like barrier that protected the town had turned

from a pearly white to a dark gray mist. I could barely see through it—just enough to make out that we were at the side street where the town met the barrier. I'd been here once before, with Moira and Orion.

The magic radiating from the barrier felt different. Dark and sick.

"This is weird. Something is wrong." Hesitantly, I reached out to touch the magical barrier. Last time, it'd thrown me backward. That should probably be enough to keep me from touching it, but I had to know.

The smoky barrier burned my fingertips. I hissed in a breath and jerked my hand away.

"My mother never mentioned anything like this. The worst thing that is supposed to happen to Elesius is that it dies because it gave me the life and magic from all its plants." And that was as bad as I could imagine. "But this is different."

I sniffed delicately, trying to get a feel for the magical signature of the evil black smoke without taking it into myself. I'd had enough dark magic lately. I got a vague whiff of sulfur and burning rubber.

Ares stepped forward, his hand outstretched. His fingertips collided with the black smoke and he grimaced, then pushed harder.

"Don't!" I reached for him.

"Wait." He shuddered, the magic clearly affecting him, then pushed his hand through farther. It only went an inch into the smoke. His brow creased.

"What is it?"

He pulled his hand back from the smoke, his muscles straining and his face reddening slightly. It took ages for him to withdraw his hand. A small bead of sweat formed at his temple, testament to the pull of the smoke. Finally, his hand popped free.

"It's essentially impenetrable," he said.

I picked up his hand and inspected it. It looked all right, at least. Strong and broad, sculpted with tiny muscles that created a topography on his flesh. "That was dangerous."

"I'm in the company of a dangerous woman," he said. "Some of that must have rubbed off."

I glanced up at him. "You were plenty dangerous before you met me."

A seductive smile tugged at his lips, just briefly, before he turned to the barrier. "This is very wrong, whatever it is."

I swallowed hard, cursing myself for the moment of flirtation. My mother and father were trapped in there. "We have to save them."

"Then we need to determine what this barrier is made of. It's a spell of some kind—a dark one. But for what purpose?"

"We need a sample of the barrier. Maybe someone can help us determine what the spell is." I called upon my conjuring power, letting the magic flow through me, and envisioned a glass vial with a cork. The bottle appeared in my hand a moment later, and I uncorked it. "Cross your fingers that this works."

I was operating on guesswork as I pushed the bottle through the smoke. Pain sliced up my fingertips as they collided with the black mist. I shoved hard, finally getting the mouth of the bottle into the smoke so that the black mist could flow into the glass. Ares was one serious badass—or masochist—for sticking his whole hand in there.

"I think that should do it." I pushed my other hand into the smoke and corked the bottle without withdrawing it from the gray barrier. When I pulled the whole thing out, the vial was full of smoke and the magic heated the glass.

Ares took my hand and kissed the back. Then he took the other and kissed it.

My heart warmed. "Are you fixing my boo-boos?"

"Boo-boos?" He frowned, confused.

It was adorable.

"You know, when children scrape their knees and their parents kiss it away?"

Understanding dawned in his eyes. "Ah, yes. Yes I am...fixing your boo-boos." A wry laugh escaped him. "If only it were that easy."

"If only." I looked back at the gray smoky barrier and the people within. What were they doing in there? Were they okay? "Then maybe we could fix them."

# CHAPTER TWO

We arrived back in Magic's Bend moments later. Cass and Del weren't visible through the windows of P & P, so they must have headed off to Dr. Garriso's office at the museum.

I turned to Ares. "We need to take the sample to Darklane. I have some friends there who can help us."

"An upstanding citizen like you, with friends in Darklane?" he said.

"Hey, I only break one rule." *Being a FireSoul.* "And I can't help that."

He nodded. "To Darklane we go."

I gazed longingly at Fabio, parked right on the side of the street, then turned to Ares. If he were willing to transport us, which he clearly was, we'd save valuable time. I reached for his hand, and he took mine, drawing me close.

The ether sucked me in as Ares transported us to Darklane. Despite it being a reasonable hour—eight thirty in the morning—the streets were dead quiet. The old Victorian buildings, which were coated in centuries of black grime, looked like they were sleeping off the bender of a lifetime.

The streets stank vaguely of dark magic, and the sun filtered weakly through gray clouds. Though it'd been sunnier back on Factory Row—and no doubt in other parts of town as well—Darklane didn't tolerate things like sunlight and fresh winter breezes. This place was trapped in the mire of dark magic.

"This way." I led the way down the narrow, cobblestoned street. Darklane was one of the oldest parts of town, and unlike the Historic District, the upkeep had been lacking.

We passed no one as we walked toward Apothecary's Jungle. The sign above the door swung creakily in a nonexistent wind.

"You're friends with Aerdeca and Mordaca?" Ares asked.

"I am."

"Brave woman."

"All of us." I began to climb the stairs. "And if they can't help us, I have another friend who possibly can. Aethelred the Seer. He lives a few doors down."

I was about to knock on the purple door when a creaky voice sounded from behind me. "I wouldn't do that if I were you. It's too early to appear without an offering."

I turned. An old man with a white beard hurried down the street toward us, a greasy paper bag clutched in his hands.

"Aethelred. Speak of the devil." I stepped down to greet the old seer. As usual, he was dressed in a blue velour tracksuit with his beard tucked into his trousers. Cass had once said he looked like Gandalf on his way to senior aerobics, and I couldn't agree more. "What are you doing here?"

"Waking the beast." He cackled and held up his bag. "Mordaca and I have a weekly date for a walk along the ocean, but she'll only get up early if I bring her bacon sandwiches."

"Mordaca?" As far as I knew, the grumpy blood sorceress didn't wake before noon. And the idea that she had a standing exercise date with the old seer? Kinda blew my mind.

"We like to gossip." Aethelred winked.

"I guess you know the best stuff, given your profession."

14

"And so does she, given her contacts." He turned sharp blue eyes on Ares. "Who is this?"

"This is my friend Ares, Enforcer for the Vampire Court."

"Ah, I see." Aethelred held out his hand.

Ares took it and shook. "Good to meet you."

At the contact, Aethelred gasped softly, his gaze riveted to Ares.

"What is it?" Ares demanded.

"Nothing. Nothing." Aethelred shook his head and stepped back, concern creasing his already well-creased face.

"You had a vision," I guessed. "About Ares."

But it hadn't been good, if his expression was any indication.

"Tell me," Ares said. "I'm happy to pay you, as I understand it is your work."

"Ah." Aethelred looked toward Mordaca's door, clearly desperate to get away from us.

"We're going there, too," I said. "So there's no escape. What did you see, Aethelred?"

The old man grimaced. "Fine. But no payment. I didn't want to see this, and I didn't go looking."

Dread chilled my fingers and toes, stretching everywhere in between. "What is it?"

Aethelred sighed and looked Ares straight in the eye. "You will lose what you love most in this world."

I gasped, my heart plummeting to my feet.

Ares's expression did not change, though his eyes may have grown slightly colder. Or maybe I was imagining that.

"What do I love most?" Ares asked the question almost like he didn't know.

Suddenly, I wanted to know the answer to that. Was desperate to know.

"I don't know," Aethelred said. "That's up to you. But beware. It will be gone. So you'd best appreciate it."

*Holy fates.* I swallowed hard, searching Ares for any sign of distress. I found none. Boy, would this dude be good at poker.

"What's taking you so long?" A smoky voice demanded from the doorway.

I turned to see Mordaca standing on the stoop, leaning one impressively curvy hip against the door. She was wearing her usual apparel—a plunging black gown that looked like she'd stolen it off Elvira, Mistress of the Dark. With her black bouffant and sweep of black eye makeup, I wasn't entirely certain she didn't take all her style cues from Elvira, straight down to the black painted claws adorning her fingertips. She looked fabulous, in a terrifying way. The fact that she was going to walk the beach in that getup made it all the more impressive. I wouldn't put it past her to wear heels.

Mordaca's sharp eyes met mine. "Why are you here?"

"We need help," I said.

She frowned, eyeing the bag of bacon sandwiches. "This is going to make me delay my bacon, isn't it?"

"I'm sorry." And I really was. If something kept me from chowing down a cheese sandwich, I'd be pretty annoyed, too. "But it's important."

"That's the real problem, isn't it?" Her dark gaze was too knowing, and I remembered how frightened she'd been of the magic contained in the beaker. She'd sensed Drakon's evil then. No doubt she'd sense something dark here as well.

"Bring them in!" Aerdeca's sweeter, lilting tones echoed from inside the house. "You're taking all day."

Mordaca beckoned us with her black-tipped fingernails. "Might as well."

We followed her into the house and through the hallway to the workshop. Aethelred trailed behind, harrumphing about the delay to his walk.

Unlike the last time I'd been there, it was silent and empty, the party having long since disbanded.

Aerdeca waited for us in the workshop, wearing her usual fabulous white pantsuit. Her blonde hair was slicked back from her head in a modern style that I didn't have the skill for but admired all the same.

Aerdeca looked at me. "You're not here for a good reason, are you?"

"No."

She frowned, drumming her white-painted fingernails on the counter. She, too, had filed them into claws, the only external indicator of how dangerous she was. People often made the mistake of thinking she was the nice sister.

*Ha.*

There was no nice sister. But they were good people, despite being scary bitches. And I meant *scary bitches* as the highest compliment.

I held up the vial of black smoke. "We need to know what kind of magic this is. It forms a barrier over a town, and the magic feels dark."

"That'll cost you," Mordaca said.

"I know." I held out my wrist. "I'm willing."

Ares pressed my arm aside. "Let me."

I shook my head. "Really. I've got it."

"No." Mordaca pointed to Ares. "Him. Vampire blood will be stronger."

"Excellent." Aerdeca smiled, though it was more a revealing of fangs. Her teeth might've been blunt, but they had the attitude of fangs. Though her sleek, white pantsuit looked out of place in the old-school witchy workshop, the feral grin looked right at home.

"It'll also cost cash," Mordaca said. "I assume you've defeated whatever evil was in the beaker and we're back to normal? The paying kind of normal, I mean."

"I doubt it." Aerdeca's brow wrinkled.

"Unfortunately, Aerdeca's right." I shot her a wry look. "Though your lack of faith stings, quite frankly."

She laughed, but it wasn't a joyous sound. "It's not a judgment of your ability, but rather the evil's strength."

"Well, you're right. He's still out there. All I managed to do was kill his mortal body. Apparently his true form is that of a big black cloud dragon."

"So basically, you're screwed," Mordaca said.

"Yeah." I nodded. "That's probably not too far off the reality."

"This'll be bad," Aerdeca muttered.

"Understatement." Mordaca gestured for the vessel.

I handed it over.

She inspected it, holding it up to the light and peering at it. "Tell me about this."

I explained the situation with Elesius and the smoky black dome. They listened intently until I was done speaking, then Mordaca turned to Aerdeca. "We'll use fire, I think."

"Agreed." Aerdeca bustled around the room, first opening the windows and then gathering silver scissors and a wooden bowl. She stood on her toes to reach the bundled herbs hanging from the ceiling and snipped some off, collecting an assortment that I recognized from my own gardening. What their magical uses were, however, I had no idea.

Mordaca gestured to Ares with a black dagger. "I'll need your blood."

He stepped forward, arm outstretched. Mordaca held an onyx bowl beneath his wrist and made a careful incision in his flesh. Ares didn't flinch. No doubt he was used to far worse. The blood dripped into the bowl.

"That'll do." Mordaca handed Ares a cloth and withdrew the bowl.

Ares pressed the white fabric to his wrist and came to stand near me. Aerdeca crunched up the herbs and poured the dust into Mordaca's bowl, then mixed it with Ares's blood. I wrinkled my nose. Blood sorcery was so not my thing.

Mordaca turned to us. "Okay, this is going to be a group

activity. The nature of spells like this—incorporeal ones—is that we have to use fire to get a sense for the magic. Otherwise, just uncorking the bottle means that we'll lose the black mist."

"What do we have to do?" I asked.

"We'll all gather around the hearth. I'll throw the vial of magical smoke in, along with the herbs and the blood, and then the spell will be revealed to us. Pay attention and let me know what you feel or hear or see. We all might have a different interpretation." She looked at Aethelred. "It's a good thing you're here. You can help with this."

Aethelred grinned, his dentures a shiny white in the low light of the workshop. "Be delighted to."

Aerdeca walked to the hearth, which lay dormant. There were no logs or other fuel, just a blank stone fireplace. She reached above the mantle and withdrew a pinch of something from a bowl, then tossed the glittery silver dust into the hearth. Flame burst to life, blue and bright. It settled down to a more normal orange, flickering in midair. I could see the stone ground beneath. Magic made this fire burn.

Aerdeca turned to us. "Gather round."

I moved toward the hearth, standing a few feet back. Ares and Aethelred joined me, standing at my side. Mordaca stepped up beside Aerdeca, the glass vial clutched in her hand.

"On my count." Aerdeca held the bowl out, clearly ready to toss. "Three, two, one."

Aerdeca tossed the herbs and blood into the flame at the same time Mordaca hurled the glass vial into the fire. The glass shattered against the ground under the flame. Immediately, the fire turned black.

Smoke began to fill the room, billowing toward me. Within moments, it had filled the air, darkening the space. My breath caught in my lungs as I tried to breathe. I gasped, desperate for air, but I got nothing.

I started to turn toward Ares to ask if he felt the same thing, but I couldn't move an inch.

Panic welled in my chest. I was frozen solid! My heart raced as I strained against the magical bonds. In front of me, Aerdeca and Mordaca stood still as ancient trees. Out of the corner of my eye, I could make out no movement in Ares or Aethelred. We were all stuck.

My heart thundered, the only part of me that could move.

Desperate, I tried calling on my magic. I had to have something that would get us out of here. But it lay dormant inside me. Dead, almost. And weaker?

Could I feel my magic at all?

The panic nearly blinded me. I couldn't move. My mind buzzed as I tried to scream, to put up any resistance at all. Nothing worked. I was fully stuck.

Around me, the smoke began to dissipate as the fire died down. Slowly, I was able to move my arm an inch. Then my leg. It took a while, but I finally broke the bonds, stumbling to my knees and gasping. Mordaca and Aerdeca fell as well, but managed to catch themselves against the hearth mantle.

I clawed at the table and pulled myself upright, turning to see Aethelred doing the same. Ares stood still as a statue, his gaze stark and his skin pale.

"What the hell was that?" I asked.

"The spell." Mordaca frowned, her brow creased.

"*That's* what the people in Elesius are feeling?" I asked.

"Yes." Aerdeca shuddered. "Hopefully not as strongly as we felt it, but they could be."

My heart ached for my family as desperation filled me. "We have to stop it. What is it?"

"It felt like a freezing spell. Definitely," Mordaca said.

"An ancient one." Aethelred leaned heavily against the table. "One that was developed hundreds of years ago."

"You can use your seer powers to read a spell?" I asked.

Though Aethelred was a powerful seer, he couldn't see all. No seer could. But what he did see always came true.

"I can. And this spell, it has a long and dark history. One that will be utilized to horrible effect in the future."

"Like right now," I said.

"Exactly." He grimaced. "That was dark, dark magic."

"How did this happen?" Ares asked. "The spell had to be intentionally cast, correct?"

Aerdeca nodded. "Yes."

"By who?" Even as I asked it, a terrifying guess rose in my mind. Though there was no proof, no evidence, and no obvious motive, it was obvious. "It has to be Drakon."

"Drakon?" Mordaca frowned. "Is that the name of the great evil that enchanted the beaker?"

"Yes. He did it, didn't he?"

"We can't say for certain," Aerdeca said. "But the magic was as dark and as evil as that which stained the beaker you brought us."

I looked at Ares. "It has to be him."

"We don't know that. But yes, it could be."

"Why, though? They must be frozen for a reason."

Ares shook his head. "I have no idea."

The others shrugged, brows creased.

"How do we stop this?" I asked.

"I don't know," Mordaca said.

"This type of spell can be cast in many ways," Aerdeca said. "Determining how it was done will help you break it. Or even learning *why* it was cast. What was the purpose? These are clues that could help."

I turned to Aethelred.

His gaze was disappointed. "I cannot see much about the spell. Only that this type of magic has been used on a small scale before —on one person at most. But this is impacting an entire village. How could such evil be possible?"

"I've felt the evil." I shuddered at the memory of Drakon's

dark magic. I'd used it to defeat him at the castle in Siberia, but it had made me sick for days.

Aethelred scrubbed a hand over his face. "As for how to stop this, you would need to ask someone far older and more powerful than me."

*Damn.* "How the hell are we going to find someone?"

"I may know someone," Ares said. "Laima. I was going to question her about Drakon, but hadn't had a chance yet."

"The Goddess of Fate?" I'd met her in the Vampire Realm during my trials. "That could work. Goddesses pretty much top the charts of ancient and knowledgeable."

"My thoughts exactly," Ares said.

I turned to Aerdeca and Mordaca. "Thank you for the help. What do I owe you?"

"Nothing," Mordaca said.

Dread curdled in my stomach. "This is the second time."

"This evil is that powerful," Aerdeca said. "We will fight this battle with you in our way. Fate will like that we do this for you. It may help."

"Thank you." I nodded my appreciation. "I'll take all the help I can get."

Aethelred sighed. "You're going to need it."

# CHAPTER THREE

After saying our goodbyes, we stepped out of Apothecary's Jungle into the watery midmorning sun. Brisk winter wind whipped across my cheeks.

"Well, that went poorly." I tugged my coat tighter around me.

"It was—" Ares snapped his head to the left to look beyond my shoulder. Shock widened his eyes.

I turned to look.

My little dragon fluttered in midair, black gaze intent on me. Though the sunlight was filtered through clouds, his scales still glittered a beautiful green. A man stepped out of the shop near the dragon, pulling up short and gazing at him. The dragon turned to look at him, then hissed. The man winced and hurried away.

"Hey, buddy." I held out my hand.

He turned to look at me. Was he a bit bigger than he had been? Only a few inches, but I was almost sure he was.

The dragon fluttered closer. The little beast sniffed my fingertips delicately, then purred.

"You have a new friend," Ares said.

At the sound of his voice, the dragon looked up. He didn't hiss at Ares, but he didn't approach any closer either. He gave me one last glance, then disappeared.

Damn.

But he'd be back. Somehow, I just knew it. At least, I desperately wanted to believe it.

"I do have a new friend." I told Ares the story of him appearing to me, omitting the part about my trove. I hadn't taken him there yet. Maybe I would soon, though.

"Never heard of anything like that. But he clearly likes you. And only you."

"Well, I like him. Or her."

Ares squeezed my hand, clearly pleased for me. "We should get started toward the Vampire Realm soon. It won't be easy to reach Laima."

"Oh no. More trials?" I didn't have the energy for a Kraken right now.

Ares grinned. "No. But the Vampire Realm is dangerous, and the shortest route to their castle is through some deadly parts of our world."

"Speed is important, so I'll take the danger."

A grin stretched across his face. "That's what I thought you'd say."

"Just let me call Cass and Del to tell them what's happened and where we're going."

He nodded, and I stepped back from the middle of the sidewalk to lean against the building. I pressed my fingertips to the comms charm at my neck. "Cass? Del?"

"Hey!" Cass's voice came through clearly. "Any luck with your mother?"

"Some, but not with the dragon. I didn't get to talk to my mother." I explained the terrible dark spell on Elesius and what we'd learned in Darklane.

"Oh no." Dread laced Cass's voice. "That's terrible."

The thought of what they were going through made my

insides coil. "We're headed to the Vampire realm for more answers."

"Damn," Del said. "More Kraken?"

"No, which is the only good news. There's a good chance that Drakon is behind the threat to Elesius."

"What?" Cass said. "Can you not get a break?"

"Apparently not. We don't know for certain, but it's possible."

"Why is he targeting your village?"

The cold dread that had cloaked me grew worse. "I have no idea."

"It could be a way of catching you," Del said.

"That's most likely."

"Which means we have to be extra wary," Cass said.

"We will be." I looked at Ares and saw the affirmation in his eyes. "You guys keep hunting for answers in this world. Every now and again, keep trying to locate Drakon."

We'd been attempting to find him with our dragon senses, but he was still blocked. Some kind of powerful concealment charm, we thought. Didn't mean we couldn't keep trying, at least.

"On it," Del said.

"Good luck," Cass added. "Be safe."

"You too." I cut the connection and looked at Ares. "Ready to get out of here?"

"Let's go." He reached for my hand and pulled me toward him.

I gripped his bigger hand and closed my eyes. The ether sucked us in, throwing us through space toward another realm.

I stumbled slightly when it spat us out in the Vampire Realm. It was night here, as always, and the moon hung heavy in the sky. The towering white arch that marked the official entrance gleamed in the dim moonlight, the rose-covered vines looking nearly black.

A screech sounded, familiar and lovely. I looked toward the sky, catching sight of the flaming red blur streaking toward me. A

Pūķi. The dragon was followed by two others. They landed in front of us in a row, eyes intent on me.

"I think they're smiling," Ares said.

I raised my arm, showing the Pūķi the protective bracelet that Ares had gotten them to make for me. "Thanks for this, guys."

They snuffled.

"I'll take that as a 'you're welcome.'" I conjured an apple for each, handing them over. The Pūķi gobbled them out of my hand, snorting their pleasure before taking to the sky.

"Ready?" Ares asked.

I nodded, glancing at him, my eyes taking in his changed features. He was the scary version of Ares that came out in the Vampire Realm—sharper cheekbones and harder eyes. More pronounced muscles and a deadlier air than when he was on Earth. And considering that he looked pretty damned threatening on Earth, that was saying something.

I followed him through the arch, my gaze moving from his features to the creepy statues that bordered the walkway. Mythical beasts stared at me—Minotaurs, hydras, and two-headed wolves all followed me with their stone gazes, ready to pounce if I put one foot out of line. A shiver raced down my spine. I was suddenly glad that scary Ares came out when we were in the Vampire Realm.

"Do these guys ever come alive?" I asked.

"They do, if they sense someone trying to enter with ill intent."

I made a mental note never to do that. "How long will it take us to reach Laima?"

"Several hours at least. Maybe longer."

"There's no Vampire cell service to just call her up?"

"Unfortunately, no. And definitely not for goddesses. We're lucky the fate goddesses choose to live in our realm, but they do so on their terms. They like their privacy, and their palace is cut off from the rest of our world. We won't have to go the long way around that we took during your trials, but the shortcut is fraught with the usual dangers of the Vampire Realm."

We reached the main courtyard where Magisteria and Doyen usually held court in their chairs. As expected, they lounged in their creepy thrones, each holding a wine goblet and chatting. They stopped mid-sentence to look at me, gazes unreadable. No greeting, but no attack either.

So it was going to be a standoff, then.

I couldn't blame them. They'd come into our relationship thinking that they were the bosses and I was just hoping to curry their favor. But now I had some fated task that Laima had commanded they help me with.

So yeah, we weren't going to be besties.

I waved, but didn't say anything. They just stared me down.

"They really don't like me, do they?" I whispered to Ares.

"They don't know what to make of you." He turned away from the courtyard, which seemed to be the central meeting place, and led me down another path. "There's no one else like you, Nix."

A smile tugged at my lips. In the distance, lights twinkled in a valley. "Is that the vampire city?"

"It is. I live just outside. We'll pick up my ride and head toward Laima."

"You can drive here? Yet you still gave me a rickety rowboat in which to fight a Kraken?"

"That's the point of a trial." He grinned, so handsome in the moonlight that my breath caught.

I shook away the sappy feelings. I *so* did not have time for that right now.

He gestured to another path, and we took it. This one wound up the side of a ridge toward a house on a cliff. Night-blooming flowers dotted the path on either side, white and sparkling in the glow of the moon. The trees were twisted and ancient. Forest creatures chirped from the branches. I really hoped they weren't

27

the Night Terrors. Those fanged black squirrels gave me the heebie-jeebies.

"Though this place is terrifying, it sure does remind me of a fairy tale," I said.

"Did you ever read the old fairytales in their original form? They could be frightening."

I smiled, then gestured toward the building that we approached. "Is that your place?"

"Yes."

"You don't like living down in the city with everyone else?"

"This is convenient. It's located near the portal, and since I spend so much time on Earth, being able to commute easily works for me."

"By foot, I assume. I can't imagine driving a car down the path between those scary statues. It would offend their ancient sensibilities, and they'd come alive and eat it."

He laughed and turned onto the drive. The house wasn't large, but the walls were made entirely of glass. The view had to be fabulous. A large modified motorcycle sat in the driveway.

I whistled. "That's no car."

The tires were huge, and the front was reinforced with a metal cage, like it could be used to ram things. It was a hulking machine built for off-roading, a vehicle like a cartoon GI Joe would ride.

"There's no driving in the civilized areas of the Vampire Realm. But for things like this, where we have to cover a lot of rural terrain quickly, the bike works well."

"You imported it with magic?"

"Yes. Motorcycle factories aren't really our specialty. This place is...ancient."

"I like ancient."

"Then you'll like it here." He climbed onto the bike and gestured for me to join him.

I boosted myself up onto the seat behind him. It'd been built for two and stood relatively high off the ground due to its large tires. The vehicle was rugged and suited to Ares.

He cranked the key that was sticking out of the ignition.

"I guess people aren't going to steal the Enforcer's bike, huh?" I shouted over the roar of the engine.

"Not likely." He reversed, pulling out of the driveway, heading farther down the road away from his house.

The breeze rustled my hair, bringing with it the scent of flowers and magic. The need for the off-roading tires soon became apparent. Within a mile, we were on rocky terrain heading away from town.

Soon, we entered a jungle. Massive trees towered overhead, silent sentries in the dark night. The screech of jungle animals echoed around us. The bike cut easily across the jungle floor, climbing over massive tree roots and winding around boulders.

"So the vampire world has a ton of different climates, then?" I shouted.

"It does."

"Like *Zootopia*."

"Zoo-what?"

"You know, Judy Hopps, bunny cop?" I was wearing a T-shirt featuring her, in fact. The bunny in question brandished her carrot-shaped voice recorder. "I love Judy Hopps. She never gives up."

"Like you."

I smiled, my heart warming. "Being compared to Judy Hopps is about the highest compliment I can imagine."

"You're ten of Judy Hopps," he shouted over the wind and engine noise.

I laughed. "Not possible."

A shriek tore through the night air, sending a shiver racing down my spine. "What's that?"

"Kamikaze Sparrow." Ares hit the gas, and the bike revved forward. "The jungle is their territory."

"That sounds like a big sparrow."

"It is."

A skeletal black bird swooped though the sky, dodging trees and heading straight for us. It was huge—about the size of a golden retriever—and about to collide with our heads.

Its beady black eyes zeroed in on me as it neared.

"Lean left!" Ares roared.

I ducked to the side as Ares swerved the bike to avoid the monster bird. We sailed by, the bike at a sixty-degree angle with the ground. The bird barely missed us. I could feel the rush of wind from its wings.

"Lean up!" Ares shouted.

I leaned up, following him, and the bike righted itself. I spun around to watch the sparrow hurtle toward a tree, out of control. It collided with the trunk, exploding in a burst of black dust. The dust dissipated to reveal a gouge in the tree trunk.

My heart leapt in my chest. "It's not a real bird!"

"Magic," Ares shouted. "Protective magic born from the jungle. Kamikaze Sparrows dive-bomb intruders."

"Cool!" And terrifying.

We zoomed through the jungle, ducking and swerving around trees and Kamikaze sparrows. My skin chilled as we nearly collided several times.

We'd just veered around one when another came from the left, about to plow into us.

A flash of red streaked by, slamming into the sparrow. The bird exploded into black dust as we sailed by. A Pūki shot high into the air.

"Thanks!" I called.

Ares laughed and drove us expertly through the jungle, weaving around trees and avoiding a panther that eyed us nonchalantly from a boulder. The Kamikaze Sparrows continued to dive-bomb us, but the Pūki kept them away.

After an hour, the jungle thinned. Ares pulled the bike to a stop in front of a great gorge. The other side was at least a hundred feet away. I peered down into the black depths. The moonlight couldn't penetrate all the way to the bottom.

I swallowed hard. "That's gotta be two hundred feet deep."

"At least. And there's nothing but jagged rocks below."

I shivered, catching sight of a rickety suspension bridge spanning the great crevasse. "Are we crossing that?"

"We are indeed."

"Indiana Jones at least got a river."

"It was full of alligators."

"Oh, yeah." I grimaced. "Not sure which I'd prefer."

Ares hit the gas and drove us along the edge of the gorge, headed toward the suspension bridge that didn't look big enough to support the bike. Growls sounded from deep below, sending a shiver across my skin.

"Are there monsters down there?"

"Probably," Ares shouted back. "Never had a chance to check for sure, but those growls aren't new."

Ares turned onto the bridge, and the bike zoomed over the wooden slats. The rickety bridge swung back and forth. There was a rope handrail on either side, but no way it was strong enough to keep us on this bridge if we veered off track. Ares's skill on the bike was the only thing keeping us from plummeting into the darkness below.

"Shift hard when I tell you to!" he shouted.

"What?"

"Left!"

Instinctually, I threw my body left. Ares did the same. Our movement forced the bridge to sway that direction right before a fireball shot up from below. The heat singed me as it hurtled toward the sky.

"Holy fates!" I shouted.

"It's coming back down!"

I looked up, watching the brilliant orange ball rise high into the sky and then plunge back down.

"Right!" I screamed.

We leaned heavily right, barely shifting the bridge. But it was just enough to save our bacon. The heat of the fireball dropping past us made my heart leap into my throat. We were *so freaking close* to being turned into flame-broiled Magica.

The wind tore at my hair as we zoomed across the bridge. Ares called out "Right!" and "Left!" every time a fireball flew toward us from below. It was like he could sense them. Then I watched them fly into the sky and called out which direction we should dodge toward on their return trip.

We were burned only once, when a fireball flew too close to our thighs. It stung like the devil, but didn't feel catastrophic at least.

I could barely breathe by the time the bike climbed onto solid ground on the other side. My heart thundered so hard I could hear it over the roar of the engine. I turned around to see one last fireball hurtle up from the depths. It barely missed the bridge, flying toward the sky and then plummeting into the gorge below.

I collapsed against Ares's back, panting. "Holy crap, your world is scary."

"No kidding." He turned around and gripped the back of my neck, pressing a kiss to my lips. "Good job back there."

"Thanks."

"Are you all right? How's the burn?"

I inspected my thigh. The denim was singed away and revealed bright red skin, but it wasn't charcoal. "Fine!"

"Good. Tell me if you want me to heal you."

*Not unless I am about to croak.* Not until I knew more about our blood connection, at least.

He turned around and revved the engine, setting off away from the gorge. This side was no longer jungle, but rather a field of waving wheat. Like the great vast fields of the American

Midwest, where Dorothy lived. The air changed scent, leaving behind the rich greenness of the jungle in favor of thunderstorms on the prairie.

The moon shined brightly upon the swaying fields of wheat. In the distance, thunderhead clouds billowed high into the sky. Lightning cracked within the clouds, far enough away that I couldn't hear the thunder. The display was fabulous, though.

Joy welled in my chest as we plowed across the field, wind whipping at my hair. Compared to the jungle, there was so much freedom here. This kind of speed reminded me of Fabio.

An old farmhouse crested the horizon, sticking up like a sore thumb. Ares veered toward the building, his big bike eating up the ground.

"Will there be help there?" I shouted.

"The opposite!"

*Great.* As we neared, a woman came out onto the porch.

Ares pulled to a stop at her front stoop. She propped her hands on her hips, giving us a considering look. Her graying hair was pulled back in a loose bun and her apron tied smartly about her waist. With her uniform and work-worn hands, she looked just like Auntie Em from *The Wizard of Oz*. There was even a dog lounging on the stoop. But he was no Toto. The little black beast had huge fangs.

He growled at me. I waved, a weak smile tugging at my lips.

"Vampire dog?" I whispered to Ares.

"Maybe." He raised a hand in greeting. "Ma'am."

"You want to cross my fields?" Her voice was more powerful than I'd expected, something you'd hear from a goddess.

"We do."

"Then you'll have to solve the riddle if you hope to reveal the path and make it out alive."

Riddles. I wasn't terrible at riddles. But what did she mean by 'reveal the path'? I looked past her house, toward the open field beyond.

But there was no more field. Just the vast nothingness of space.

Well, crap. We'd definitely have to solve this riddle now.

"Of course," Ares said.

Thunder rolled in the distance. The massive clouds neared us.

The woman's eyes glowed brightly, an eerie sight, and she recited her riddle. "I go, brave and roaring across the earth, burning buildings and houses in my wake. Smoke rises from the fires as I leave in a trail of disruption and death. I have the power to shake tall trees until their leaves fall down, covered in water, and scatter exiles far from their lands. What am I?"

I frowned, searching my memory. What the hell was she? Thunder cracked in the distance, making it hard to focus. My mind raced as the woman began to tap her foot. Tension thickened in the air, stress from the riddle and the oncoming storm.

"There's a time limit," the woman said.

"We're thinking." Ares turned around to look at me. "Any luck?"

My mind spun like a hamster wheel as I thought of things and discarded them. What the hell was she talking about? One wrong guess and we wouldn't get through, so I had to be sure of my answer.

The thunder boomed, growing closer and making it hard to concentrate. We'd be rained out, struck by lightning before we fixed this.

An idea flared. "This riddle is supposed to help us cross and avoid dangers?"

The woman nodded, her magic glowing eerily. "It is."

The thunder cracked again. Understanding dawned. "It's a deadly thunderstorm. The lightning leaves the fires, and the wind shakes the trees. The rain drowns everything and drives people from their homes."

The woman inclined her head. "You'd best hurry across, then."

I looked past her house to where there'd previously been

emptiness. There was now a waving field of wheat, just like the one we'd crossed.

Ares nodded his appreciation, and tore off across the valley. The storm rolled toward us, thunder at our backs.

"Good job!" Ares shouted.

"Go faster!" I turned around, eyeing the clouds and lightning roaring toward us. High above, the moon disappeared behind the clouds, sending the night into darkness. Vicious lightning strikes illuminated the dark sky. Droplets of cold rain splattered against my face.

"We can't outrun it!" Ares shouted. "Watch for the lightning."

Oh, holy fates. I was the lightning spotter? My skin chilled with fear, and I turned around to study the clouds. The problem with lightning was that it was impossible to see it coming. It just struck and burned.

Thunder deafened me as I squinted toward the clouds. Lightning struck a hundred meters away, but there'd been no freaking clue that it was about to hit.

Rain poured from the sky, and we raced across the field. Pūķi flew alongside us, high in the air. They gathered in certain areas of the sky, darting across the clouds like groups of birds.

After a moment, I realized that they clustered right where lightning was about to strike, no doubt drawn by the energy. Rain blurred my vision as I kept my head tilted upward to observe them. When they clustered right above us, my heart rate spiked.

"Go left!" I screamed.

Ares dodged the motorcycle to the left just as a bolt of lightning struck the ground where we'd been. I laughed, crazed and relieved.

As we tore across the prairie, I kept my gaze glued to the Pūķi. Every time they gathered right above us, I shouted to Ares, and he diverted our path.

My heart raced and my body buzzed with adrenaline as we

narrowly avoided our death countless times. When the rain finally stopped and a massive castle on a hill appeared on the horizon, I was just about out of energy.

"Oh, thank fates." I collapsed against Ares's back, holding on for dear life.

He drove us up the hill leading to the gates of the castle. It was the same fabulous white stone structure from my trials. The three pennants still flew from the towers—gold, silver, and opal. I now knew that there was one each for the goddesses of fate.

The blue water in the moat glittered clear and inviting. I looked away, remembering what Ares had said about it dragging a person straight to the center of the earth.

"Well done, you two!" a voice called from above.

I looked up at the parapets. Laima leaned over the edge, Karta and Dekla at her side. Their magic hit me hard—Laima's crashing wave signature, Karta's thunder, and Dekla's electricity. Each held a cocktail in one hand and a pair of binoculars in the other. Laima's golden hair was studded with opals that glittered in the moonlight.

"Do you make people go the hard way so you can watch them?" I shouted, remembering Laima's obsession with reality TV. Anything to stem the boredom of immortality.

"We do!" She laughed. "Clarence will show you inside."

The drawbridge lowered, and the massive castle gate lifted, revealing a handsome young man in a black suit. He couldn't be more than twenty-two, with the fresh-faced appeal of a clothing model who sold expensive tank tops to teenagers.

"You're the butler?" I asked.

"Intern." He gestured us inside.

What the heck kind of college credit was he getting out here?

Ares drove the bike into the main courtyard and cut the engine. I climbed off, limbs still shaking from the stress of the motorcycle ride through hell.

"Would you like to freshen up?" Clarence asked.

"Oh, my fates, yes." My wet clothes were chilling in the night air.

He led us through the flower-filled courtyard toward the entrance into the castle. This was the back entrance, I realized. Though the gate had been similar, this area was smaller. Still filled with flowers, but more intimate.

We entered the castle through the back. The impressive door and massive great foyer screamed luxury and style. Antique furniture contrasted wonderfully with modern art done in swirls of blue and silver. Clarence led us up a wide, curving staircase. I felt like Scarlet O'Hara, but wetter and dirtier.

We followed him to a door at the end of the hall, which he pushed open to reveal a fabulous bedroom of gold and blue. He grinned, white fangs glinting in the light of the chandelier overhead. "There is a bathroom in the back. Take your time, and the goddesses will meet you when you are done."

"Thanks." I entered, longingly eyeing the bed. It looked like a pile of heaven, but it'd be a long time before I slept.

A door beckoned from across the room. I hurried toward it and gasped when I stepped inside.

The whole place was gold, with gems set into the light fixtures above. It scattered the light into rainbows. It was both gaudy and glorious. My FireSoul tugged hard, roaring up at the sight of all these riches.

I turned to Ares, who'd just entered. "Can you believe this place?"

He glanced around, bemused. "It's quite…something."

So he wasn't as big a fan of the sparkly sparkly, but I *loved* it.

Clarence appeared in the doorway behind Ares, a tray in his hand. Crystal wine goblets glittered in the light, and a tray of fancy sandwiches made my mouth water.

I licked my lips like a hungry hound. "That was fast."

"I want full credit." He set the tray on the counter.

"What internship is this?"

"Business administration."

"Hmm." I frowned at him. "I think the goddesses are taking you for a ride."

He grinned. "I know. But have you seen them?"

They *were* pretty fabulous. I could see why Clarence didn't mind hanging around here for the summer, hoping to get lucky.

"Enjoy your stay." Clarence smiled and disappeared. The bedroom door clicked shut.

"Smart kid."

Ares grinned. "Out of his league."

"Yeah, but hope springs eternal." I went to the tray and picked up a goblet, sipping the golden liquid inside. Flavors exploded on my tongue, fruity and sweet and sparkly. My head immediately started to buzz. "This is amazing."

"Ambrosia." Ares sipped his own, eyes going heavy lidded. "Drink sparingly."

"Or what?"

"All kinds of things. And we need our wits about us here." He handed me a sandwich. "We can expect help from the goddesses, but also tricks. They are bored, and we must be wary."

I bit into the sandwich, my eyes rolling back in my head. I had no idea what the delicate little thing was made of, but holy fates, was it tasty. I scarfed down four more and polished off my Ambrosia, then turned toward the showers.

I desperately wanted to jump into one of those fabulously large showers, but Ares was here. We weren't exactly at the *get naked together* phase of things. There were also two shower stalls, however. Enough for both of us. Though I might *briefly* entertain the idea of sharing, now was not the time.

"I'm getting in that one." I pointed to the glass door on the right. "You can have the other."

"Fair enough."

I grabbed a fluffy white towel from the counter and went into the shower stall. It was as big as my bathroom at home, the walls entirely covered with pearls. I tapped one with a fingertip, my FireSoul roaring. Yep, they were real.

And this was the guest bathroom? I couldn't imagine where Laima showered.

Quickly, I cranked on the water and then tugged off my soaking clothes, tossing them over the shower door. The warm water soothed the stress from my muscles as I buried my head beneath it. My mind drifted, carried on a wave of Ambrosia. Steam twined around me, making me feel like I floated on a cloud. The water pounded away at my shoulders, sending me into a trance.

Distantly, I heard the water turn on in Ares's shower. He was naked. In this room. With me.

My breath escaped me.

*Whoa.*

Visions of him in the shower raced through my mind, followed quickly by all the things I could do if I slipped out of my shower and into his. I felt so good and relaxed and carefree right now that the idea felt pretty genius really.

I shivered with anticipation as I reached for the shower door handle.

# CHAPTER FOUR

My fingers closed around the door handle when an errant thought popped into my head.

This was all too amazing to be true. The gorgeous bathroom. The wine, the food, the fluffy towels, and the butler/intern.

The bored goddesses.

Ares was right. That Ambrosia was dangerous stuff.

I scowled, head still swimming from Ambrosia, and looked around. Was there a video camera in here? I didn't spot one, and couldn't imagine that the Vampire Realm could accommodate that level of technology, but maybe goddesses wouldn't need video cameras to spy.

Either way, I wouldn't put it past them.

So I turned away from the door. Away from Ares. "Are you trying to make your own dirty movie, Laima? Because I'm not falling for it!"

There was no response, but I flicked her the bird anyway for good measure. Maybe they didn't see it, but it made me feel better. And I wasn't going to worry about them when I had this amazing shower to enjoy. Just because I wouldn't be sharing it with Ares didn't mean it wasn't awesome to shower inside a pearl-encrusted wonderland.

I scrubbed my hair and sobered up a bit before I turned off the water and wrapped a towel around me. I peeked out of the shower stall to see if the coast was clear. It was, so I stepped out.

"Don't come out yet!" I called, carefully averting my eyes from the glass door enclosing Ares's shower. It was frosted, so I couldn't see much, but I didn't need any more temptation than the goddesses had already provided.

Quickly, I conjured some fresh clothes. This time, I went for a Keyboard Cat T-shirt. For good measure, I conjured Ares an identical set of clothes to the ones that he'd soaked. Hopefully I got the sizing correct.

"All clear!" I called to Ares before going into the bedroom. I ignored the fabulous bed in favor of the large window. It overlooked the courtyard below, where the Pūķi still lounged, eating from golden plates that Clarence was currently refilling with sliced fruit.

"I wonder if he's really getting college credit for this," I muttered.

An orchid on the windowsill leaned toward me. I petted the stalk, feeling the magic inside the plant. My new powers were crazy. No question, I definitely needed to find time to practice.

Ares joined me a moment later, wearing the clothes I'd conjured for him and scrubbing a towel over his hair. "Ready to find the goddesses?"

"Yep." I turned to him. "This place is pretty but it's dangerous."

"Keep that in mind. I like Laima, Karta, and Dekla, but they're powerful, bored, and entitled. It's a dangerous combo for mere mortals such as ourselves."

"An understatement." I followed him out of the room, descending the stairs to the main foyer. I was just about to call out for Clarence when he appeared, a friendly smile on his face.

41

"I shall take you to their Fabulousnesses." He gestured toward a hallway.

I grinned. "That's a mouthful."

"It is how they prefer to be addressed today."

"Today?" Ares asked.

"Glory as great as theirs cannot be described with only one title."

"These ladies are nuts," I whispered to Ares.

"That they are."

"I like them anyway."

We followed Clarence down the wide hall toward a door at the end. He let us into a luxurious movie theater. Three huge chairs sat in front of the screen, each housing a goddess. Laima wore slinky ivory pajama bottoms and a top, both of which shimmered like diamonds. Dekla was dressed in torn jeans and a golden bustier that made her dark skin glow. Karta lounged with her legs thrown over the side of her chair. Her bodysuit glittered like silver lightning, and her dark hair fell like water over her shoulder.

I looked toward the movie screen. Instead of Ares and me on the screen, it was Bree and Ana, the badass girls from Death Valley. They were driving their buggy across the valley once more, fighting off a huge monster made of black smoke.

"Why are you watching them?" I asked.

Laima turned, eyes sparkling with interest. "They're fascinating! Do you see how they attack that beast? They're untrained, but the sheer ferocity!"

Ana was driving straight for him, and Bree was on the roof of the vehicle, her arms outstretched to shoot her magic toward the monster. "They're impressive. But should you be spying? And how are you doing it?"

"It's our one great luxury." Laima waved a hand, and the image disappeared. "We're not going to quit now."

42

I laughed. "Given the bathroom that we just showered in, that can't be true."

"Just gems and gold. Nothing very interesting. Not like them."

My dragon soul disagreed. "We were hoping you could help us with some questions."

Laima leaned back in her chair, gaze thoughtful. "I thought you might be returning."

"For help with your great task," Dekla said.

"We were actually waiting," Karta said. "Took you long enough."

"You were waiting for me?"

The three nodded, then spoke in unison. "We had a vision."

"You did? What was it?"

"In good time." Laima waved a hand, and two chairs appeared in front of theirs.

They were big and comfy, and I was relieved to see that Laima wasn't playing some stupid power trick by giving us tiny kiddo chairs. She'd never struck me as the type, anyway.

"Tell us what has happened since you were here last," Laima said. "I'd like to know where you stand before we discuss what we three have seen."

Ares and I sat. The words poured out of me. I told them all about the magical enchantment surrounding my village and Drakon.

The three goddesses leaned back, their expressions thoughtful. Karta even tapped her chin and pursed her lips.

"So you believe this Drakon is responsible?" Dekla asked.

"Yes. Though I don't know why."

"Hmmm." Laima leaned toward Karta and Dekla. All of the goddesses looked worried, their brows creased.

"This may be the great Dragon Killer," Laima murmured.

*Ah, crap.* Did she think I couldn't hear her? Because I could, and her words scared the hell out of me. I didn't know what the Dragon Killer was, but it definitely sounded *bad*.

"Do you really think so?" Karta asked.

"I do." Laima kept her voice low. "Given what we saw in our vision, it is obvious."

"I can hear you, you know," I said.

Laima startled, then looked at me. She sighed. "Of course. It's just that this is a dark vision, one that we foresaw but... Frankly, it scares the crap out of us."

"Drakon is the Dragon Killer," I said.

"It sounds like he is, yes," Laima said. "I had this vision many centuries ago. It's been so long that I hoped it would never come to pass. He is the greatest threat the world has ever known. But the vision came again three nights ago."

That was when I'd killed Drakon's human form and released the shadow dragon. No coincidence there.

I leaned forward. "Up until now, we assumed Drakon wanted to hurt the dragons because his magic felt so evil. But you're confirming that he wants to kill them."

"Yes," Laima said.

"Then they can't be dead as most people thought," Ares said. "They're hiding."

Excitement shivered across my skin. This whole thing was terrifying—but the idea that dragons might not be dead?

*Awesome.*

"Do you know why he wants to kill them?" I asked.

"No," Laima said.

Karta and Dekla also shook their heads.

"We have to save them," I said. Which meant finding them. But they were so well hidden that my dragon sense couldn't find them. "But we don't have much to go on. And whatever we have, Drakon already knows."

"What do you know?" Laima asked.

"There's a prophecy. I learned it a few days ago, after he did. 'Deep in the place where the earth meets the sun and the mist meets the magma, the Phoenix will give rise to the dragon's return, or the Triumvirate will engender their fall.'"

Laima stood and began to pace. "I haven't heard that whole thing before, but I have heard the first part somewhere."

"It's part of an ancient Norse myth," Karta said. "Long ago, my mother told it to us. You may wish to focus your search there."

My heart leapt. A *location*. True, it was a whole country. Several countries, actually, considering that the Norse had spread their influence and religion across the north Atlantic. But at present, the whole world was our searching grounds. This narrowed it down tremendously. "Thank you."

"It is not a problem." Karta shook her head, eyes faraway. "If this Drakon is the Dragon Killer, we need to help you."

"She is fated for great things," Laima said. "You know I've seen this."

"I just wish you could see if I would succeed," I said.

"That, I cannot do." She frowned. "But I do have something for you." She went to a table at the back of the room, picking up a short sword and returning to me. She held it out. "This is for you."

"Me?" I took the short blade, which was encased in a scabbard connected to a leather strap. I drew the blade out of the scabbard. It was only about two feet long, but it was perfectly weighted in my hand. The blade was shining steel and the hilt wrapped in leather. "Why?"

"Part of my vision said that you must have this. The Blade of the Fates will cut through anything. *Anything*."

"Wow."

"You will need this in your coming task. I don't know for what, but it is important that you keep it with you at all times. Use it only when you are certain it is necessary."

"Of course." I slipped the blade back into the scabbard and slung the strap over my chest. The blade sat at my back, as comfortable as if it'd been made for me. The short size made it a convenient way to carry the weapon.

"Good." Laima smiled. "That is all we have for you. Should you need our help again, just ask."

"Can you help us return to the main part of the Vampire Realm without going back the hard way?" I *really* didn't have the energy to go back through the lightning fields.

Laima nodded. "We can. Let us walk you out."

Karta and Dekla rose from their plush, La-Z-Boy thrones and the three goddesses escorted us down the hall. Karta and Dekla immediately surrounded Ares, showering him with compliments. Karta squeezed Ares's bicep, and I almost growled.

"Down girl," Laima said to me.

"I have no idea what you're talking about." I kept my tone haughty.

"Mmmm-hmmm. Sure." She winked at me. "But there's something there between you two. I've never seen him like this before. He's a changed man. No longer cold and aloof, but riveted by you."

"Yeah. There's something between us, but I don't know what yet."

"How can you not know? Seems pretty obvious to me."

I frowned. "I had his blood. A lot of it. It's created some kind of connection between us, and I'm afraid that it's the reason we've grown close, not our true feelings." Actually, I was pretty darned sure my feelings were accurate. It was Ares I was concerned with. He was so powerful and handsome and good. And if he liked me as much as Laima said? *Wow.*

Laima gave me a quizzical look. "Really? The blood connection has made you able to sense his emotions? And he can find you in return?"

"Yes. But it didn't happen to my *deirfiúr* when he gave her his blood to heal her several days ago."

"That's the normal course." Laima smiled. "But you and Ares are fated. That's why you have the connection through his blood."

"What do you mean fated?"

"In vampire lore, this type of connection comes around once in a millennium. The fated ones, a couple destined to be together. They'd fight time and the stars to align their fates with one another."

"That's us?" I shivered, both delighted and horrified. That was *huge*. "What about a few great dates and eventually a lifetime of happiness? Isn't it kind of insane for fate to get involved?"

"It doesn't mean you can't have those things, too. Or that you shouldn't. You still need to fall in love. But I'm telling you that if your symptoms are accurate, then fate certainly wants you to be together."

"Wow." I stared at Ares's broad back. Him and me...forever?

~

The goddesses were able to make us a portal to anywhere in the Vampire Realm, so we chose to return to Ares's house. They escorted us down to the courtyard where we'd left the motorcycle and the Pūķi.

Ares and I stopped in front of the bike, and the Pūķi came up to join us. Laima stopped a few meters away, holding her hands out to create the portal. Golden light shined from her palms as she drew a large circle in the air. The space glowed bright and beckoning.

Ares and I were about to climb onto his bike when I asked, "Can I drive?"

"Sure." Ares grinned. "Ever driven through a portal before?"

"No, but I can figure it out."

"All you, then."

I looked at Laima, Karta, and Dekla. "Thank you for the help. And the sword."

It still felt natural on my back, as if it'd always been there.

"Anytime." Laima waved.

We climbed on the bike, and I cranked the engine. It roared to life, and the Pūķi made excited trilling noises. I gunned the engine and drove toward portal, the three Pūķi zipping alongside us.

As soon as we entered, the ether sucked us in, and my head swam. When it spat us out in Ares's driveway, it took all I had to keep the motorcycle upright and drive it toward the driveway. I parked and cut the engine.

"Whew!" I climbed off. "That was short but sweet."

The Pūķi plowed out of the portal behind us, their bright red forms illuminating the darkened driveway.

Ares led us toward the front door of his house. A fluttering sounded from behind me. I turned. My newest dragon friend had appeared out of the air. He was now even bigger—roughly the size of a sheepdog. He fluttered up to the three Pūķi, his red wings glinting in the moonlight. Though his body was shaped like theirs, he looked very different. They were made of flame, but he had scales like a regular dragon.

The Pūķi sniffed him, and he sniffed them back. A loud purr rumbled from his chest.

"Hey, pal." I approached. "You like your new friends?"

He turned to look at me, his black eyes calm and happy. Thank fates. I didn't know how to break up a dragon fight if things didn't go well with this group. The Pūķi watched as my dragon approached me, his gaze held fast to mine.

"Be careful," Ares murmured.

"I will."

He was right to be cautious. The dragon was an unknown species of mysterious origin. But he was mine. I could feel it.

I held out a hand, and he snuffled it, his breath warm on my palm. "Do you breathe fire?"

48

He turned his head and expelled a little trill of flame. I laughed. Cool!

"Are you hungry?" I conjured an apple—the Pūḵi's favorite food—and held it out to him. He ignored it, but the Pūḵi voiced their interest.

Voracious beasts.

I conjured two more apples, then tossed one to each of the three Pūḵi.

"Well, it seems you don't eat, fella."

He purred.

"And you understand me?"

He purred again, then flew so close that I could reach out and touch him. I did, petting his head. Warmth and magic flowed up my arm.

"Whoa." I pulled my hand back and looked at Ares. "I think he gave me strength."

The dragon purred.

"Do you know anything about this kind of creature?" Ares asked.

"Nothing. Just that he appeared earlier today."

"Del and Cass don't have them?"

I glanced at him. "No, why?"

He lifted a shoulder. "They're FireSouls, too, so I thought they might."

I grew still. Not scared, but alert. "How did you know that? I've never told you that."

"No, but I'm observant."

"Yeah."

He reached for my hand, squeezing. "Their secret is safe with me."

I nodded. "I know. It's just...I'm always going to worry about them, you know?"

"Yes. More than yourself. That's how family works." He gestured to my dragon. "And now you have new family."

I grinned. "I do."

I didn't know much about the care and feeding of dragons, but since he didn't eat and he kept disappearing, I figured he could take pretty good care of himself. And the idea that he might be giving me more strength or magic or whatever? Crazy.

I reached out to pet him again, but one of the Pūḳi made a high-pitched trilling noise. My dragon whirled around to face him, body positively vibrating. With excitement?

The Pūḳi shot into the air, doing flips and loop-de-loops. My dragon darted after him, joining in.

"Looks like I've been deemed boring," I said.

"They do like to play."

All three Pūḳi and my own special dragon darted around the trees in a game of chase that I didn't understand. But they seemed to be having a good time, and exhaustion pulled at me, so I turned to Ares. "How about we get some sleep? It's pretty late."

"Good idea." He led the way in through the beautifully carved wooden door and flipped on a light.

The golden glow spread over the open space, revealing a welcoming living room with a fabulous view over the town. "You're partial to city views, I see."

"Coincidence." Ares headed toward the left corner of the house. "This was my parents home. I didn't choose it, but I do like it."

"Me too." I followed him into a beautiful old kitchen. The cabinets were carved with glorious tree designs. "Those are incredible."

"My father made them. He was a woodworker."

"Wow." I inspected the artwork as Ares dug into the fridge. He pulled out a bottle of wine and some blocks of cheese, quickly creating a tray that made my mouth water. "How did you know I could go for some of that right now?"

"Call it instinct." He ginned and handed me a glass of red wine. "Sorry, I have no bourbon."

"That's okay. This is more date-like."

"Is this a date?" Pleasure suffused his voice.

"Um, it could be." I raised my glass. "Wine and cheese paint a pretty clear picture as far as the movies are concerned."

He clinked his glass with mine. "A date it is."

I followed him out into the living room. He set the plate on a table in front of the couch, then took a seat. The couch faced the windows instead of a TV, providing a fabulous view over the valley beyond. Spotlights illuminated incredible metal sculptures. They were modern, yet relatable. Though it was hard to say what they all were, they each gave off a different emotion—joy, sorrow, humor, pain.

I walked toward the window. "Those are incredible."

"Thank you."

I turned back in time to see Ares's cheeks darken so slightly I wouldn't have noticed if I weren't attuned to him like he was the weather channel during a hurricane. His face was still sharp and dangerous, but that was definitely a *blush*. And it was sexy as hell.

"Hang on, did you *make* them?"

He cleared his throat. "I may have."

"So your father was a woodworker, and you are a metalsmith?"

"Something like that. And my mother built small boats. We are good with our hands, I suppose."

I grinned, and just barely resisted making a terrible joke. I joined him on the sofa, snagging the biggest slice of cheese from the plate and popping it in my mouth. I chewed and swallowed. "How do you find time for a hobby?"

"Not easily. I fit it in during late nights, usually. Otherwise, my work with the council keeps me busy."

"I can see how that would be."

"You must have something besides working in your shop and saving the world to keep you busy?"

"Well, there's not as much working in the shop as I'd like these days." Ancient Magic had been closed for over a week now, ever since we'd deemed Drakon Threat Number One.

"You'll get back to it."

"I do have a hobby, though. Gardening."

"Given your most recent magic, that fits you well."

"Thanks. It's a pretty impressive place, my....garden." I'd almost said trove, but stopped myself. He probably knew I had one, but I wasn't yet ready to share it with him. Almost. But not quite.

"I'd love to see your garden one day."

My jaw dropped as the worst sexy pun ever flashed in my mind. Ares raised a hand to his face, pinching the bridge of his nose. I laughed. I didn't even need to see his face to know that he, too, got the unspoken joke.

Laughter bubbled out of me, so I tried quieting it with a bite of cheese. It worked pretty well, as it usually did.

"I like you, Nix."

I smiled at him. "I know."

"Don't get sappy on me now."

"I like you, too." I set down my wine glass. "I've been worried that I like you *because* of the blood bond we share."

"That's never happened with anyone else."

"I know. And I asked Laima about it. She said that we're fated." Just the idea made me short of breath. I did like him—so much. I just didn't want fate getting its sticky hands into my life. It'd done that enough already.

Ares laid a gentle hand on my arm. "Hey, are you all right?"

"Yeah. Totally." I tried to still my racing heart.

"Well, you look a bit stressed."

"Ha, you read me well." I drew in a shuddery breath. "I guess I am. Fate—while I believe in it—has also decreed that I must fight a monster of incredible strength and power. The greatest threat the world has ever known, according to Laima. I don't exactly want fate getting involved in my romantic life, too."

"It doesn't have to be that way. Fate has indicated a preference, but we can still do what we want."

"We can." Shakily, I pushed an errant lock of hair away from my face. What I wanted to do was kiss him.

As if he could read my mind, Ares's gaze riveted to my lips. My breath caught at the heat in his gaze. He leaned in, giving me enough time to shift back or say no.

Of course I didn't. I'm not an idiot, after all.

He pressed his lips to mine, warm and firm. I moaned, reaching out to wrap my arms around his neck. He gripped my waist, pulling me toward him as I devoured his kiss.

The heat of his muscles seared me, making my head spin. I wanted *more*. So I took it one step farther, climbing onto his lap and pressing myself full against him. Pleasure shot through me and I gasped.

He groaned, a desperate sound that made heat spike in my blood. His strong arms wrapped around my waist, crushing me to him as his lips trailed skillfully from my mouth to neck. He shuddered and passed over the sensitive place, no doubt because he didn't want to be too tempted.

*Bite*, I wanted to command. But it was crazy. What little sense I had left told me that.

So I pressed my lips to his neck instead, tracing my tongue over the smooth, hot skin. A moan escaped him, driving me crazy.

Tapping sounded at the window. I jumped, pulling my lips away. Ares stiffened, suddenly alert. His gaze darted to the windows at my back. I turned.

Three Pūki and my dragon all sat at the window. My little beast had tapped the glass with his claw.

"Holy crap, the kids caught us," I said.

Ares laughed.

I was about to lean back into his kiss when my dragon tapped again, this time more frantically. Worried, and also a little bit annoyed, I climbed off of Ares and went to the window.

Concern glinted in the dragon's dark eyes. At least, that's what I guessed it was.

"I'm okay, buddy."

He shook his head, dark eyes still dismayed. I almost felt like saying "What is it, boy?" the way that kid would say to Lassie when she came to the farm with a warning about a boy who'd fallen down a well.

"Something is wrong," Ares said.

"Yeah." The Pūki looked pretty clueless, bless their hearts. But my dragon was *definitely* trying to tell us something. "As exhausted as I am, I think we need to head back to Magic's Bend."

My comms charm didn't work here, so there was no way to call home. That left the old-fashioned way—inter-realm space travel.

# CHAPTER FIVE

It was an exhausting walk back to the entrance of the Vampire Realm. By the time we reached the marble platform at the entrance, though, I was nearly running. My dragon had led the way, his haste making me even more nervous.

We stepped through the portal, arriving in Magic's Bend a moment later. The streets were dead quiet this late at night, but the lights to P & P were blazing golden onto the dark street.

"Something's wrong." I raced toward the cafe, my dragon at my side. P & P was never open this late, and Connor wouldn't keep the lights running after hours.

As I expected, a group of people sat within. Cass, Del, Connor, and Claire, along with two people that I couldn't recognize from the back.

I hurried in, Ares behind me.

Cass and Del looked up, stark gazes relieved.

"We couldn't reach you on your comms charm," Del said.

"I was in the Vampire Realm."

"Of course. I forgot it doesn't work there." Worry glinted in Cass's eyes. She gestured to the newcomers, who had turned around.

One had messy, short blonde hair and wore burnished red leather armor. Dark circles filled in the space under her eyes. The other was short and slight, a dark-haired woman with large glasses and timeless features.

"Corin. Fiona." I stepped forward. "What's wrong?"

"There's been a kidnapping at the League of FireSouls. Two days ago," said Corin, the blonde woman.

The League of FireSouls was the only organization of Fire-Souls in the world. They lived in a hidden realm a bit like Ares's, all thirteen of them holed up in a castle that could accommodate far more. They were like a magical Justice League, protecting FireSouls from persecution and danger. Cass, Del, and I had known them for months, but they'd never come to us for help.

If Fiona, the ancient fae librarian, had deemed it necessary to leave her beloved library, it must be bad.

"Who was kidnapped?" I asked.

"Alton." Corin's voice cracked.

I thought of the handsome, dark-skinned warrior who wore the same style armor she did. He was a good guy—and powerful as hell.

"He's been gone the last three days." Fiona's voice held the ancient, timeless quality of one of the fae.

"How'd they get him?" I asked.

"We don't know," Corin said. "Nor do we know who it was. We've been trying to find him, all of us using our dragon senses, but we've had no luck. We were hoping that you could try. You three are the strongest FireSouls we know."

"Of course we'll try." But holy fates, the timing was crappy. We couldn't divert from our mission to stop hunting Drakon and the dragons, but no way could we let our friends down either.

I looked at Cass and Del, reading the same thing in their eyes. I wasn't even sure we *could* help. While it was true that we were powerful FireSouls, able to find almost anything, we'd had a hell of a hard time locating Drakon or the dragons. We definitely weren't infallible.

"We'll do everything we can," I said. "But since you're here, could I ask you some questions about something that is troubling us?"

Both Corin and Fiona had a well of knowledge we didn't. Fiona, especially, since she was the librarian at their castle compound.

"Of course," Corin said.

I took a seat, my bones weary. Everyone else sat as well. It didn't take long for me to spill the whole story. Fortunately, the FireSouls were used to weird stuff and could keep up. Even better, they'd have our backs no matter what.

"Dragons," Corin murmured. "Really?"

I nodded. "Do you know anything about where they might have gone when they disappeared? I thought they'd died out, but I was wrong."

"Most people thought that." Fiona's gaze took on the distant quality that it often did when she was visiting the resources in her mind. "When they disappeared five hundred years ago, no one knew what to make of it. Eventually, legend said that they died. But no one found any bones."

"Are there any records?"

"None." Fiona shook her head. "Just an oral history compiled by a scholar in the seventeenth century. The only thing that he could determine was that there were three primary dragons. As large as houses."

I shivered at the idea, delighted and horrified.

"The last time anyone mentioned seeing them was in Norway," Fiona said. "Six hundred years ago."

Excitement jumped inside me. Laima had mentioned that the prophecy was an ancient Norse one, and there had also been a sighting.

That was too much to ignore.

"We've had FireSouls hunting the dragons for centuries," Corin said. "In addition to our goal of protecting other FireSouls, it is our mission to find them."

"Except we never have." Fiona frowned. "Never even come close."

"In the five hundred years since they disappeared, you've made no headway?" I asked.

"We discovered the clue about Norway, but nothing else. They're magically protected, we think, and they're hiding so well that even we couldn't find them."

"Frankly, most of us have given up hope," Fiona said.

I frowned, hating the sentiment. "We're going to find them."

"I hope you—" Corin's gaze darted behind me.

I turned. My dragon had appeared, hovering in the air.

"What is that?" Corin's voice echoed with awe.

"My dragon."

"He's far too small to be a natural-born dragon," Fiona said.

"I don't think there's anything natural-born about him." I held out a hand, and the dragon flew up to give me a sniff. Then he nuzzled his head against my hand. My heart fluttered.

"May I?" Corin tentatively raised her hand toward the dragon.

"You can try."

Corin smiled and held her hand out. The dragon sniffed her, then ignored her, turning his attention back to me.

"Sorry about that." I felt a bit like a mother whose child wasn't shaking hands with newcomers. But if my dragon had boundaries, I was going to respect them.

"When did you get him?" Fiona asked. "How?"

I told her all I knew, which wasn't much. "He just appeared one day" was pretty vague. While we talked, Connor brought out drinks for everyone. He handed me a glass of Four Roses, and I sniffed the whiskey appreciatively, then drank.

The dragon flew closer, sticking his head toward my glass. I held it out so he could smell it better. His red tongue darted out, lapping up some of the whiskey.

"He likes whiskey!" Delight rang in Del's voice.

"I guess so." Though I could be worried about him becoming intoxicated and flying into a tree, he was a fire-breathing mythological creature built of magic and mystery. I doubted a little whiskey was going to hurt him.

"This is very unusual." Fiona's eyes took on a distant gaze, the way she did when she was remembering something she'd read in her library. "I recall reading something about familiars for particularly gifted FireSouls. It's possible that he is your familiar."

"Like a witch's familiar?" I petted the dragon's head, feeling that familiar frisson of power streak from him to me.

Fiona nodded. "Yes. He could help emphasize your powers. Make them stronger—make *you* stronger."

Excitement raced through me. "He did. At least, I feel a little stronger every time he touches me."

"That's amazing," Del said.

Could I use this gift to find Drakon or the dragons? If we had an extra boost of power, maybe our FireSouls could latch onto him. Or at least find some answers.

I turned to the little dragon who was now perched on my chair's armrest. "Could you help me with my powers later tonight?"

His head inclined as if he were agreeing, so I decided to take that as a yes.

Maybe we were finally getting somewhere.

"Thank you, Corin and Fiona." I smiled gratefully at them. "We'll do all we can to find Alton."

"No, thank you. We really need your help." Corin reached inside her bag and pulled out a long dagger. She handed it to me. "That was his. Perhaps it will help you find him."

My fingers closed around the metal hilt.

Corin stood. Fiona followed, her gaze on me. "Take care of your familiar, Nix. You're lucky to have him."

"Do you know anything about feeding him? Or taking care of him?"

"No. That information is long gone with time. I'll check my library, but I can't promise anything."

"Thank you." We said goodbye to them, and they hurried out into the night, headed back for their realm.

I turned to everyone. "Feels like we're finally getting somewhere, huh?"

"I'm feeling a little hopeful," Cass said. "About the dragons. Not Alton."

Guilt sent a rush of heat to my cheeks. "Of course. Alton. I'm too focused on the dragons."

"No, you're just worried about Drakon. That's normal." Del's eyes were kind.

"No excuse. We have to find Alton. He's helped us so much. All of the FireSouls have."

"There's no question you need to hunt for answers about Drakon," Cass said. "I'll look for Alton with Aidan."

"I'll go wherever you need me," Del said.

"With us, I think." I looked at the clock. It was two in the morning. "Let's get some rest and start early in the morning."

"What about us?" Connor gestured between him and Claire.

"Thank you, guys. You're lifesavers. Since we're currently in recon mode, why don't you hang out here? I'm sure the fight will come soon enough."

Connor and Claire grinned, two identical smiles.

Everyone said their goodnights. Ares stopped me at the door, and I turned. "I'm going to go back to the Vampire Realm tonight. I need to..." He hesitated and I filled in the words for him.

"Eat? Or drink, I guess it is?"

"Yes."

"I don't mind, really." I leaned up and kissed him. "I'll see you tomorrow."

He kissed me one last time, then disappeared.

I joined Del and Cass on the sidewalk. The dragon floated at their side, watching me.

"He's a good guy," Del said.

"Seconded," Cass added.

"Thanks, guys." Their approval meant a lot.

We set off down the quiet sidewalk. The night was cold and dark as we walked past the golden street lamps. The dragon flew overhead, just a few feet above me.

"Where are Aidan and Roarke?" I asked.

"Off following a lead from one of Roarke's contacts at the Order of the Magica," Del said. "But they're headed back here because it didn't pan out."

"Damn." I stopped in front of our green door and unlocked it. The dragon led the way up to my apartment. It was surreal to stare at his little butt and tail as he flew up. I turned back to look at Cass and Del behind me. "Can you believe this?"

Del grinned. "I really can't."

"You deserve a dragon buddy," Cass said. "But you do have to name him."

"Good point." I said goodnight to my *deirfiúr* and headed into my place, the dragon fluttering in behind me.

I tried to get him to eat something from the kitchen, but he refused, showing no interest in the food.

"Your loss, pal." I chomped on the cheese sandwich I'd been trying to lure him with and went into the bedroom.

I saw him eyeing the bottle of Four Roses on the counter.

"You little lush."

He blew a little stream of fire from his nose. It looked like a happy motion.

"I'm going to shower quickly. Make yourself at home—and that doesn't mean burn things."

He blew out another little stream, and I crossed my fingers as I made my way into the bathroom. I made quick work of the shower, then went into the bedroom to change. The dragon was curled up on the pillow next to mine. He was so big that he covered the whole thing, but he seemed determined to sit there, like a cat balancing on a cushion.

"Comfy?" I asked as I tugged on PJs.

Thankfully, he didn't blow any fire out of his nose. I hoped it was because he realized the bedding was flammable.

Once dressed, I climbed into bed and leaned against the headboard, then turned to the dragon. "What do you want your name to be?"

He gave me a steady look, but said nothing.

"How about Jeff?" I asked.

He seemed to like it—at least, he didn't light my bed on fire. So he'd be Jeff.

"So, Jeff. Will you help me with my magic?" I hovered my hand over his back. When he didn't object, I laid my palm on him. Magic shivered through my flesh.

"Wow." The sparkle of power ran up my arm and into my chest, settling there like a light. "You really do make my dragon sense stronger."

He wiggled deeper into the pillow, content to hang out while I joined my magic to his. With his power flowing through me, I called upon my dragon sense. I thought of Norway and the dragons and the answers that I wanted there. The prophecy.

A tug pulled around my middle.

*Norway.*

As I'd thought. There would be answers there.

I removed my hand from Jeff's back and lay down next to him. "Night, Jeff."

He purred.

~

Early the next morning, a pebble clicked against the window in the living room. I hurried toward it, peering out. Ares, as expected.

I pushed open the glass and leaned out. "We really need to get you access to the building."

"Anytime." He grinned, so handsome that I swooned a bit.

"I'm coming down."

A few minutes later, after I'd strapped my new blade to my back, I let him into the building. He leaned down and kissed me, making my thoughts go temporarily blank. I wrapped my arms around his neck and leaned up to get a better taste.

"Take it inside, you two."

I turned at the voice. Cass pounded down the stairs from above. Aidan towered behind her, a grin on his face.

I scowled at her, then sighed. She was right. This wasn't the place or the time. As much as I wanted some time alone with Ares—heck, a whole week—we had more important things to be doing.

"You're going after Alton?" I asked.

She patted the bag hanging over her shoulder. "Yep. Got his dagger right here. We're going to grab a bite to go before tracking him down."

"If he's in a bad spot, get backup first." I tapped my comms charm. "We'll be there in a heartbeat."

"Will do." Cass gave me a quick hug and hurried out.

"Good luck." Aidan gave a little wave as he left.

"You too." I turned to Ares. "Let's head up. Del and Roarke are supposed to meet us here."

Ares followed me up the stairs to the apartment, where Jeff sat on the couch, his little butt on the seat and his back pressed against the cushions. His white belly gleamed with a pearlescent sheen.

"He looks comfortable," Ares said.

"Yeah. Jeff's really adjusting well."

"Jeff?"

"It suited him. I had a friend named Jeff once. Coolest kid I ever knew. A park ranger."

"Jeff it is, then." Ares held up a paper bag from P & P that I hadn't seen before. No doubt because I'd been attached to his lips.

I sniffed, my stomach growling. "Are those cheese scones I smell?"

"Of course."

As usual, Jeff paid no attention to the food. But I paid more than enough attention for the both of us, chowing down. In the long run, it was best that Jeff was fueled by magic instead of food. I had no idea how to potty-train a dragon.

A knock sounded at the door. Del's distinctive pattern.

I swallowed the last bite. "Come in!"

She let herself in, followed by Roarke. Both were dressed for a fight, in dark winter clothes. It'd be cold where we were going—Norway in the winter was no joke—but brightly colored sportswear would do us no favors. We didn't know what we'd be going into, but it was always best to be prepared to blend into the shadows.

"Are we ready to do this thing?" Del asked.

"We are." I glanced back at Jeff, who'd fluttered off the couch as if he were ready to come along. I didn't know how good the little dragon would be in a fight, and if it came down to that—which it often did on our trips—I hoped he'd stay safe.

"I can transport us there in two trips," Ares said.

"Sounds like a plan," Roarke said.

Though Roarke could transport using haunted places and graveyards, we weren't heading towards either of those. And while he had a badass power to break through the ether and create portals, it took a good bit of magic to do so. Best to save our strength for any fights we might get into.

"To Trondheim," I said. "I can only tell that we need to be in Norway, and at least Trondheim is a supernatural city."

"So we won't scare the crap out of a bunch of humans." Del grinned. "I like it."

Ares held out his hand, and I took it. Del took his other hand. A moment later, the ether sucked us in, pulling us through space and spitting us out in Norway.

# CHAPTER SIX

We appeared in front of the soaring edifice of a massive church. It was beautiful, built of ornately carved gray stone and surrounded by skeletal trees. The sun sparkled high overhead. It was three o'clock, and since it wasn't a Sunday, the churchyard was empty.

The cold was bitter and bright, biting at my nose and cheeks. The sun would set soon, but there was no way to avoid that during a Norwegian winter.

"I'll be back." Ares returned to Magic's Bend to get Roarke. Jeff hadn't transported with us.

I turned to Del. "Here's hoping this works."

She knocked on her head and crossed her fingers—Del was the most superstitious person I'd ever met—and I mimicked her movements before calling on Jeff.

Frankly, I had no idea what I was doing, so I just imagined him coming to me, calling him with my mind.

At first, there was nothing. *Jeff! Come on, Jeff! We're in Trondheim.*

A moment later, the little dragon popped our of thin air, hovering nearby.

"Hey, buddy." I smiled.

He blew out a stream of fire, which I took to mean *hello.*

"Come on over here." I gestured and he flew toward me, stopping in midair. I placed my hand on his warm back and he purred. I gasped as magic flowed into me, strong and pure.

Del watched, eyes bright, as I called upon my dragon sense, drawing energy and magic from Jeff. He seemed to have an endless well of the stuff.

There were so many things I wanted to know that the questions jumbled over one another in my head. *Where are the dragons? Where is Drakon? What is the place where the mist meets the magma?*

At first, my dragon sense was slow to latch on, as if some of the questions couldn't be answered. Some things were protected even from Jeff's magic. Even our powers combined couldn't break through certain protection charms. But eventually, I got ahold of something. The tug was firm and strong, pulling us toward the southwest.

Ares appeared out of the air with Roarke.

I removed my hand from Jeff's back. "Right, we've got to get moving again. We're close, but not close enough."

"Where to?"

"Sognefjord. The entrance on the sea." I'd read up on Norway this morning, just a quick browse of Wikipedia so that I'd recognize things. The Sognefjord was one of the largest fjords on the western coast. I looked at Jeff. "You go wherever it's safe, okay? Back to my place or something."

I knew it was silly, trying to take care of a magical dragon that could pop out of space in a moment, but he was my buddy now. I really liked Jeff, and he wasn't exactly the biggest dragon.

Jeff just gave me a look that said, *I do what I want.*

I scowled at him.

"Let's go." Ares held out his hand, and I took it. Del did the same.

Within a minute, all four of us were standing in a valley at the edge of the fjord. Snow-covered mountains rose high on either side of us, glittering white in the sun. The water of the fjord was a dark contrast, and on the other side of the long deep bay, more mountains reached toward the sky.

To our right, the fjord spilled out into the Norwegian Sea. To our left, it traveled hundreds of miles, deep into Norway.

"Well, this is desolate," Del said.

"That's the truth." I turned, studying our surroundings and focusing on my dragon sense for a clue. It'd been clear that this was where we should come, but now that we were here... What, exactly?

Magic sparked on the air, an unfamiliar signature that prickled against my skin. A warning. I spun in a circle, warily inspecting our surroundings. My friends did the same, each as tense and ready.

About fifty meters in the distance, a small patch of snow exploded into the air. I jumped back. "Holy crap!"

Ares shifted into a fighting stance, his eyes alert on the now falling snow. Del and Roarke's magic swelled, as if they were getting ready to shift into their more dangerous forms.

When the snow settled, a small man stood in the valley. Stocky and no more than four feet tall, he had a long beard and dark clothing.

He waited patiently, as if we were supposed to go to him. And why not? He'd just popped out of the earth like one of the giant killer worms from *Tremors*.

Hopefully he was less dangerous.

"Who the heck is that?" Del whispered.

"No idea." I approached slowly, my friends at my side.

As we neared, I realized that the man's clothes were an old-fashioned style, with suspenders and big heavy boots. He wasn't wearing nearly enough to combat the elements out here, but he didn't seem bothered.

"You trespass upon the land of the *dvergr*. What is your

purpose?" His voice was deep and hoarse, that of a much bigger man.

I glanced at Del and whispered, "What are *dvergr*?"

"Dwarves, I think. In Old Norse. Live underground and are great metalsmiths."

I turned back to him. "We seek passage up the fjord."

"Harrumph." He crossed his arms over his chest. "Only a boat of the ancients shall take you up this fjord lest you be eaten by the Kraken."

I grimaced. More Kraken? I'd gone my whole life with no Kraken, and now there had been two in less than a month?

"What is a boat of the ancients?" Ares asked.

"What it sounds like." The *dvergr* gestured to the valley around. "You must find the boat in this valley and pay the boat's owner to take you to the fjord. It is the only way you will make it alive."

"Why are you helping us?"

The *dvergr* grinned, revealing stubby little teeth. "Payment, of course." He dug into his pocket and withdrew a shining orange stone. Amber. The Vikings had loved amber, right? "This is what you must give to the ferryman to pay him. It is enchanted. But you must pay me for it first."

I could feel the magic of the amber. No way I could conjure one of my own to pay the ferryman. It was clearly a special stone. So I'd need to bargain. "What do you want?"

His grin widened in a face that only a mother could love. "You must make the decision and the offering. If I accept, the stone is yours. If I don't..."

The ground around us rumbled as magic sparked on the air. More of the prickling sensation. The snow exploded around us, thousands of white clumps flying high into the air. The world whited out and I tensed, calling on my magic.

When the snow settled, over a hundred dwarves stood around us, all grinning. Each carried a beautiful weapon. All were blades

—swords, daggers, and axes—and all were intricately designed and crafted. Truly beautiful works of craftsmanship that the dwarves no doubt hoped to remove our heads with.

"Those are some bloodthirsty grins," Ares murmured.

He was right. I looked at our *dvergr*. "I really don't want to fight you all."

"You do not. So you must make your offering." He raised the gleaming stone. "And take your prize to be on your way, far from the realm of Svartalfheim."

"Sounds good." I held up a finger. "Just give us a moment to discuss how to best present our gift to you."

He grinned, a greedy gleam in his dark eyes. I swallowed hard and turned to my friends.

"These *dvergr* mean business," Roarke said. "What shall we give them?"

"I have no idea." I looked at Del. "What have you read about dwarves from Norse myth?"

"Nothing much. They live underground in their city of Svartalfheim—we don't want to go there, trust me. They spend most of their time crafting beautiful metalwork."

I glanced at the weapons surrounding us, each so beautiful that they almost made their dwarf masters look good, too.

The dwarf who held our gem made a noise in his throat, clearly ready for us to get this show on the road. I glanced at him and realized that unlike his counterparts, he did not have a weapon.

I looked at my friends. "I've got an idea."

"Do it," Ares said.

I grinned and called upon my magic, envisioning the most beautiful blade in my own personal collection. It was a dagger of the finest steel, made in Japan by a master craftsman hundreds of years ago. I used my conjuring gift to recreate the blade in its exact form. It appeared in my hand, perfectly weighted and sharper than those knives on late night TV that could cut through pennies.

I turned and held it out to the *dvergr*. "Does this suit your tastes?"

His eyes gleamed bright as he gazed at the blade. "Indeed it does."

He reached for it, his hand small and gnarled. I yanked it back and held out my hand. "The gem first, please."

"That is not how it works," he said.

"It is now." I hardened my voice. "I insist."

He frowned, clearly waffling. What was the big deal? Had he not intended to give me the stone? Was this a game?

A cunning glint entered his eyes as he gazed around at the other *dvergr*. They eyed us all avidly, all but licking their chops.

*Ah, hell.* These guys really weren't going to play fair. And they weren't even subtle about it.

Ares made a sound low in his throat and caught my eye. I glanced at him. He raised his brows and nodded toward the *dvergr* nearest him. The short man with a bushy brown beard and eyes as brilliant as emeralds was edging closer to us, his hand gripped tightly around his broad ax.

Yep. Ares agreed that we were in a pickle. A shiver ran down my spine. We couldn't fight a hundred *dvergr*. Though they were small, they were stocky with muscles and armed to the teeth. And we couldn't bail either—we really did need to get up the valley, and he might be right about us needing a boat.

"You're planning to betray us," I said.

"I am not," he blustered, his gaze riveted to the dagger I'd conjured.

"You are." I held the knife up. "You want this. Bad. But you also want some entertainment—or whatever. I honestly don't know what you'll get out of killing us. But your buddies are all but licking their chops."

He scowled at them, as if they'd let the cat out of the bag. Mythological creatures were always so tricky.

"Why don't you just attack?" I asked.

He bristled. "Honor. We started this as an honest trade. We will finish it as one."

But they'd be happy to attack *after*. "Then here's what we're going to do. My friends and I are going to find this boat you speak of. If it's really there, then I'll believe you. We'll make the trade, and we'll be on our way."

The *dvergr* all grumbled, sounding like a low rolling thunderstorm. The one in front of me vacillated, looking between his buddies and the dagger in my hand.

He licked his lips. "Fine. You find the boat, we conduct our business."

"Good. Keep your men off us."

He grumbled.

I looked back at my friends. "Let's find this boat."

"This'll be tense." Del eyed the *dvergr*, who eyed her right back. "Scariest Easter egg hunt ever."

"I'll search from the sky." Roarke's magic swelled on the air. The gray tornado of light whirled around him as he shifted into his demon form. His snow gear disappeared, and his skin turned dark gray. Massive wings flared from his back, and he launched himself into the air.

As he circled overhead, I inspected the valley around us. It was hard to see anything except the dwarves standing in the now-lumpy snow, all of them gazing at us.

I called on my dragon sense, envisioning a boat floating on the fjord and asking it to help me find the vessel.

"I don't feel anything," Del said. No doubt she was trying her dragon sense, too.

"Same," I said.

"It could be hidden in the snow, or by magic," Ares says.

"If it's magic, we're in trouble," I said.

Roarke landed next to us. "There are no harbors or towns visible. Not a single living thing."

"Dang." I looked at the dwarf. "Are you screwing with us?"

He shook his head.

We all studied the valley. Chill wind whistled through the fjord. The air was silent save for the wind and the breathing of the ancient dwarves. It was so quiet here, so abandoned, that it felt like no one had been here since the Vikings themselves.

*Oh!* The errant thought triggered an idea. "Maybe the boat is underground. The Vikings were famous for boat burials."

Del grinned. "Oh, you're right."

This time, I tried asking my dragon sense to find me a boat burial. A very different thing, indeed. Particularly considering that after one thousand years underground, the boat would be in pretty poor shape. Poor enough that it might not even resemble a boat anymore.

The fact that a broken down old boat wouldn't get us up the fjord was a concern for another time.

Immediately, my dragon sense latched on, pulling me east. I pointed. "That way."

"I feel it, too," Del said.

We tromped through the snow, weaving around the dwarves who refused to move.

"Napoleon syndrome on these guys, huh?" I whispered.

Ares chuckled, but he stayed alert, ready to fight at the slightest hint of attack. It was the most uncomfortable search I'd ever conducted.

"Feels like we're just waiting for them to get bored and attack," Del muttered.

"Exactly." My dragon sense screamed inside of me and I stopped, pointing downward. "Here."

I conjured some shovels and passed them around. The *dvergr* came to stand next to us, his gaze riveted to the dagger still in my hand.

"Keep an eye on the dwarves." Ares began to dig, his vampire speed blowing the rest of us out of the water. He cleared the snow and cut through the dark dirt below. After a few feet, I touched his arm and he stilled. "Slow down, champ. We don't want to hurt the boat."

Besides the fact that it was supposed to be our ride through the fjord, it was still technically an archaeological site. Fast digging was always bad.

"There'd better be some serious magic down here," I said to the dwarf. "Because there's no way this boat will be seaworthy, and I'm not going to destroy a site just to take a bath in the fjord."

He scowled. "I am no liar."

"Yeah, you are."

He didn't even bother looking chagrinned.

I turned to the task at hand and began to dig. My dragon sense could almost sense the energy of the site as we neared it. "We're getting close."

We slowed our shovels. After about six feet, the tip of my shovel hit something slightly squishier. "We're there."

I conjured a trowel and got on my hands and knees in the dirt, uncovering a lumpy form that was clearly different than the dirt around it.

"I've found the bow of the boat," Ares said from behind me. "Or the stern. Impossible to say."

"The boats were identical at each end." I stared at the lumpy form that I'd uncovered, then leaned back on my butt, discomfort welling inside me. "Well, fates. That's a body."

"The warrior who was buried with his ship," Del said. "He'll be our ferryman."

His body was wrapped in a dark fabric that was crusted with dirt. He'd definitely decayed over the years, but how much was hard to say without removing the cloth.

"Well, I officially feel like crap about this." Though there was great scientific value in excavating graves, the way we'd done this made me feel like a grave robber. I looked up at the *dvergr*. "You better be right about this."

"You found the boat, didn't you?" he groused.

"We did." I held out my hand. "The gem, please."

"What about my dagger?"

"Let me try the gem. If I don't give you the dagger, you can kill us anyway. There are plenty of you."

He waffled, then handed over the gem. The stone was warm beneath my hand, vibrating with magic.

I held it over the body. "Um, here is payment for a ride up the fjord."

I felt crazy as a loon, but once magic started to fizz on the air, sparking with golden light, hope lit in my chest.

The lump in the soil didn't move, but the golden sparkles coalesced on top of it, forming the shape of a man. I scrambled back from the body, climbing out of the burial pit with my friends.

The golden lights faded to reveal a man dressed in ancient Viking armor. His tunic was a brilliant red, emblazoned with a golden dragon that matched his flowing golden hair.

For one surreal moment, I pictured Fabio from the old romance novel covers. But this guy wasn't quite real. He was very slightly transparent.

"Who wakes me from my slumber?" His gaze traveled over my friends and me.

"I do." I stepped forward. "We would like you to take us up the fjord to the other end."

A broad grin stretched across his face. "Ah, I wake to fight another day!"

"Not fight!" I held up my hands. "Just a ride."

His smiled stretched wider as he ignored me and climbed out of the pit. He hovered his hands over the pit, and golden light sparkled on the air, floating down into the dirt. My breath stopped short as a massive Viking ship rose from the ground, held aloft by the golden sparkles.

"Holy fates." I watched the ship float through the air toward the sea. It traveled the thirty meters and settled onto the water without a splash. The water was deep enough that the boat could sit right next to shore—almost a natural harbor.

"The real boat is still in the ground," Del murmured.

I turned and looked where she was pointing. She was right. The lump of the body was still there, and so was the end of the boat that Ares had found. We'd merely woken the ghost and a shadow of his boat. The dirt that we'd removed from the ship burial was flowing back into the grave, covering the ship right back up.

"I have no idea what's going on," I said. "This magic is crazy."

A hand tugged at my sleeve, and I turned to look. The *dvergr* stood next to me, brow furrowed. "Payment!"

I hesitated. What if the boat didn't work?

"This is surreal!" Roarke shouted.

I looked up to see him standing on the deck of the semi-transparent boat. Yep, this magic was *crazy.*

"Fair enough." I handed over the dagger.

The *dvergr* grabbed it, his eyes gleaming. His compatriots let out a victorious roar and charged, their weapons raised.

Shit. I'd been right.

"Come on!" I sprinted, Del and Ares at my side. The *dvergr's* feet thundered on the ground as they raced us. My lungs burned as I raced for the boat. A quick glance behind showed the dwarves gaining, their grins wide and bloodthirsty.

I turned back and pushed myself harder. An ax thudded into the snow at my left. It'd avoided my thigh by only inches. My heart pounded as I neared the boat and leapt on board. The momentum nearly sent me across the deck and into the fjord on the other side, but Roarke caught me. A half second later, he caught Del, too. Ares jumped on board and managed to keep himself upright.

"Let's go!" I called.

"Be gone, you foul *dvergr*!" The Viking warrior waved his arm at the dwarves.

"Grab the oars!" Ares shouted. He grabbed a huge one and used it to push the boat away from the rock ledge of the shore.

I scrambled on the deck, dodging stacked boxes and even a wagon in my attempt to find an oar. I grabbed one and hefted the heavy thing, finding a seat on one of the chests and fitting the oar against the oarlock.

From the shore, the dwarves shouted and waved, faces angry and red. Though they could throw their weapons at us, and some even looked like they wanted to, they clearly weren't willing to part with their beloved blades.

Del plopped down on the chest next to me and heaved at her oar. In front of us, Ares and Roarke sliced their blades through the water.

"Well done!" The Viking called from the stern, where he was operating the rudder. "I am Sven the Almighty!"

"How does he speak our language?" Del asked.

I shrugged and pulled on my oar. "Magic, I guess."

"Thank fates for magic." Del leaned over and peered at the ground. "Because I can kind of see the water beneath us."

I leaned over and looked too. My stomach dropped. She was right. The boat was only slightly transparent, but I could still just make out the water below. "This is nuts."

"Hoist the sail!" Sven called.

I looked at Del and shrugged. "Anything's better than rowing."

We stowed our oars and followed the Viking's orders, hauling on ropes as the big square sail rose up the mast. A crest of a dragon decorated the middle of the sail. The wind caught the fabric and filled it, pushing the boat along. On either side, the massive cliffs of the fjord soared overhead.

"This is amazing!" Del called.

"It really is." Ares stood beside me, the wind ruffling his hair. "What's in all the boxes, though?"

I looked at the boxes sitting all over the deck. There was even a cart and a loom. "They're grave goods. The Vikings included all kinds of valuables with their ship burials. Sven must have been important."

I turned back to look at Sven. He stood at the stern, the rudder handle in his hand and the wind whipping his blond hair back from his face. He looked delighted to be back on the fjord.

"Let's go ask him questions about the past," I said.

"Sure." Ares turned and we walked back toward the Viking. We'd almost reached him when he grinned broadly and shouted.

"Ahead! The fight awaits!"

I turned. We were rounding a curve in the fjord, but right ahead, I could make out over a dozen boats on the water. All were Viking boats, their long low hulls distinctive. None of the sails were raised, and they were all way too close to each other.

Shouts and screams echoed through the fjord.

"A Viking battle," Ares said.

"Holy crap, are we in the past?" Del asked.

"I don't think so." I ran toward the bow to get a better look.

Some of the Viking boats were attempting to ram each other, while others sat still in the water as Vikings leapt from one boat to another, their swords raised. Spears flew and men fell. We might not have been in the past, but that battle looked pretty real.

And we were headed straight for them.

My stomach lurched, and I turned back, catching sight of Sven's bright gaze as he steered us toward the fray.

"No!" I screamed. "Go around! We can't fight them!"

"But the battle awaits!"

# CHAPTER SEVEN

Fates, he really was like that dude Thor from the superhero movies. Just happy as a clam to charge into battle. And we'd hitched a ride with this guy?

"We paid you to take us to the end of the fjord, not to a battle!" I shouted.

He leaned into the rudder handle, ignoring me.

For fate's sake. I looked at Ares. "Did you see where he put the gem?"

"In the pouch at his waist."

"Get it."

Ares grinned and nodded, using his superior speed to race across the deck and pluck the pouch from the Viking's waist. He darted back toward me. Behind us, the sounds of the battle grew closer.

The Viking glared at us, rage reddening his face.

"You'll get it back when you deliver us to the other side of the fjord," I said. "Go *around* the battle!"

He grimaced, then nodded, turning the rudder and pulling on a line so that the sail shifted. The wind caught it and turned us on the water. I spun to face the battle.

*Shit.*

"We're too close!" Del cried.

The warships were only a hundred meters away. Several of the Vikings yelled and pointed. One of the vessels veered away from its fight, the oarsmen pulling with all their might as they cut across the water toward us.

"They'll try to ram us!" Sven shouted. There was glee in his voice.

Nutty as a squirrel was our Sven.

From the bow of the approaching boat, warriors fired their arrows at us.

"Duck!" I called.

My friends dove behind boxes and the wagon as the arrows plowed into the water twenty meters away from our boat. I scrambled across the deck and grabbed one of the shields that was hanging over the side of the boat. Everyone followed.

We huddled behind our shields as the oncoming boat approached.

"Should we row or fight?" I asked. Outrun or overpower?

We all peeked over our shields at the oncoming boat.

"I'll row," Ares said. "Two oars."

I eyed the massive oars that were built to be used one at a time, but Ares could handle it. With his superior strength adding to our sail power, we had a shot.

"Roarke and I will fight," I said. "Del, you guard the Viking. If he gets killed, we're screwed."

Del nodded and scrambled across the deck toward the Viking, her shield deflecting arrows. She adopted her Phantom form, turning blue and transparent. Any arrow that attempted to hit her would fly right through.

Immediately, Roarke took off into the air, his wings carrying him toward the approaching vessel.

Quickly, I conjured a long shield with shoulder straps and

handed it to Ares. "Wear this on your back. I'll try to keep you covered."

He nodded and shrugged it on, then stood in the middle of the boat and picked up the oars, slotted them against the oarlocks, and pulled with ferocious strength. The boat shot through the water.

The screams of the Viking battle grew louder, along with the clanging of swords and the thud of boats colliding with each other. Wind whipped my hair away from my face as we cut through the fjord.

Adrenaline surged through my veins, and I conjured my bow and arrow, then moved toward the side of the boat. The whole edge was lined with shields. I crouched behind them and eyed my target.

The Viking longship was only fifty meters away now. Roarke dive-bombed it from the sky, grabbing bowmen and throwing them into the icy water of the fjord. Their shrieks echoed through the valley.

I took aim and fired for the pilot who stood at the stern, clutching the handle of the rudder. My arrow pierced his neck, sending him flying backward. One of his crewmembers shouted and abandoned his oar, lunging for the rudder as the boat veered off course.

I aimed for the new pilot, taking him out on my second shot. Another replaced him.

More arrows flew toward us as oarsmen abandoned their posts on the enemy vessel and took up the long-range attack. Arrows thudded into the wood around me. A dozen of them poked out of the shield on Ares's back, making him look like a porcupine as he heaved at the oars.

I continued to fire at the pilots, killing one after another. It was a grisly game of whack-a-mole. I called upon my plant magic, reaching deep in the fjord to find kelp that could come to my aid. But it was too deep, hundreds of feet below.

"We're pulling away!" Del cried.

She was right. Ares's strength and our sail were beating out the now-smaller numbers of men on the approaching ship. In the distance, the other vessels still fought, but they weren't coming after us.

Roarke continued to dive-bomb the Vikings in the boat, deflecting their arrows with his shield while he yanked them off the deck with his other hand.

A quick glance at Del showed her with a shield full of arrows and our unharmed Viking pilot.

The enraged shouts of the pursuing Vikings echoed in the fjord. Finally, we were far enough away that they ceased their pursuit. Roarke left them immediately, flying toward us. He landed on the deck with a thud. Ares laid down his oars, face streaming with sweat. Blood seeped from wounds at his thigh and upper arm.

"Never thought I'd be in a Viking sea battle," Ares said.

"That makes two of us." Roarke inspected a puncture wound at the side of his bicep.

Del approached, eyes concerned. I conjured a cloth bandage and handed it over. She bound Roarke's wound.

"Are you all right?" I pointed to Ares's wounds. He'd been sliced where the shield hadn't protected him.

"Fine. They're minor and they'll heal soon."

I looked at Sven. "Why'd they come after us?"

"The crest on my sail is recognizable. They know this vessel is laden with treasure."

I studied the enemy ship as it limped back toward the battle. "Thank fates it didn't catch us."

The Viking laughed. Along with my friends, I collected the arrows that stuck out of the wooden boat and piled them in the bow. Any one of us could have been skewered like a shrimp on a barbecue.

"We don't have much sunlight left," Ares said.

I studied the sky, which was already turning pink. Winter in Norway was really not the ideal time for a mission like this. If the cold didn't get us, the darkness could. Who knew what could hide in the shadows here?

The sounds of the battle dissipated as we sailed away, cutting quickly over the smooth, dark water. The wind was chill and fresh as the sky turned a brilliant orange and pink with the sunset. It'd be romantic if we hadn't just escaped a Viking sea battle. Hell, maybe it was more romantic *because* we'd just escaped a Viking sea battle.

I glanced back at Sven. A broad grin stretched across his face. Clearly, the Viking was happy to be back on his beloved fjord.

We sailed for two hours as stars sparkled high above. Bright moonlight glittered on the dark water, the moon illuminating the fjord.

When a sharp scream rent the night air, I jumped and whirled to face Sven. "What was that?"

His eyes were wary as he searched the fjord. "Draugen. A monster. The spirit of a drowned man who haunts those on the fjord. He'll try to—"

Thunder cracked, cutting off his words. Snow sprinkled from the sky above, a frozen storm that brought with it massive waves that rocked the boat. Wind whistled through the valley. I clutched the mast, looking around frantically.

Del clung to the side of the boat, Roarke at her side. Ares kept his footing, no doubt aided by his vampire physicality. The boat rode huge waves, plunging down into troughs with a bang.

"Take down the sail!" Sven roared.

Wind and snow whipped my face as I struggled to follow his command. I fumbled with the lines, Ares at my side. We'd just managed to lower it a bit when the wind tore right through the linen. It flapped in the air, shreds waving. Quickly, we lowered the yard. It slammed down and we dragged it off the mast to stow it on the deck. I shoved my end into the bow, near Del. Ares aligned his in the stern.

"To our right!" Roarke roared.

I spun around, searching the water for whatever Roarke pointed toward.

At first, it just looked like a massive lump on the surface of the sea.

"What is it?" Del asked.

She and I stood together at the bow, clinging to the raised stempost, the elegant curving structure that was the most characteristic feature of Viking boats.

I squinted, finally able to make out some detail. "It's a huge man. Rowing half a boat."

"Half a boat?" Ares shouted.

"Yes! And he's rowing right for us!"

"Draugen will try to take us to the bottom," Sven shouted. "Everyone row!"

We scrambled for the oars. But before Del and I could make it toward the midsection of the boat, a wave crashed over the bow, sweeping us off into the sea.

Icy water closed around me, shocking me into panic. The cold froze my muscles and sent icicles through my brain, like the worst ice-cream headache imaginable. I gasped, sucking in water.

Panic almost blinded me as the dark water surrounded me.

*No!*

I kicked, clawing for the surface. I wouldn't be bested by panic. The water felt like Jello, but finally my head broke the surface. I gasped and coughed, searching blindly for the boat and my friends. Snow fell through the darkness, and waves rose and crashed all around me.

Terror greater than any I'd ever known seized my chest.

Then I saw him. Roarke, in the sky, his dark form held aloft by his glorious wings. He was searching, his head darting around.

He pointed at me and shouted. "There!"

Then he dived, away from me. I prayed he was going for Del. I shook uncontrollably as I kicked frantically to stay afloat, swallowing too much water. A moment later, a strong arm wrapped around my middle.

"I've got you!" Ares shouted.

"I can help!" I was weak, but not beaten. Together, we kicked. I followed his lead. In the sky, Roarke carried Del. We followed his figure back to the boat. By the time we reached it, I was nearly numb. Roarke helped drag us in.

I lay on the deck, coughing and sputtering.

"Draugen is coming!" Sven shouted. "Get up and row!"

*Row?* Like this? I was half frozen to death.

"Get up and fight, or he'll take you back into the water!" Sven roared.

That was all it took. The memory of the icy fjord sent a bolt of adrenaline through me. It was so strong that it jerked me to my feet. I was clumsy from the cold, but couldn't feel it.

Draugen was closer now, only fifty meters away.

"Stay low to the deck!" Ares shouted. He ran for the oars, tossing one to Roarke and one to Del. "Hold him off with your arrows, Nix!"

I nodded, shakily conjuring my bow and racing to the stern. I took up position near Sven, whose face was set in lines of concentration and worry.

"He won't like fire," Sven said. "No one on the sea does."

I nodded sharply and conjured a flaming arrow. My numb arms shook as I drew back on my bow and fired. The arrow sailed through the air, landing laughably off course. Adrenaline might give me strength, but it didn't give me skill.

I conjured another arrow and fired again. This one almost hit Draugen, who was now only twenty meters away.

"You must do better!" Sven leaned on the rudder's handle, directing us away from a large, oncoming wave. The boat rocked beneath me.

Frustration warmed me as I conjured another arrow and fired. This one hit Draugen's boat. He roared his rage. Bolstered, I conjured another, firing for the massive man.

It landed on his chest, but he swatted it away.

*Crap!*

"He's too big!" I shouted. "My arrows can't pierce."

My mind raced. I needed another plan. He was so close now that I could make out the seaweed that draped from his huge form. He was a proper monster, all right.

*The seaweed.*

Hope flared in my chest, and I reached out for the weeds, letting my life magic flow from me. *Come on, come on.* Just barely, I could sense the smallest bit of life left in them. Through the snow and the wind, I sent my magic toward the vines, commanding them to constrict around the monster.

He was now only fifteen meters away, close enough for me to see the moonlight glinting off his dark eyes. His face was twisted in a scowl, and he hauled at his oars. Waves crashed around him.

*Tighten.* I commanded the vines to squeeze him. He faltered, his oars stopping.

Was it working?

*Squeeze.* My magic sparked inside me as I commanded the weeds. My heart thundered., Finally, they did my bidding, wrapping around Draugen and slowing his movements. He yelled, thrashing against the bonds.

"Row!" Sven roared. "We're losing him."

I kept my magic flowing to the vines as my friends hauled at the oars. We pulled away from Draugen. He sat, a lame duck on the water and thrashed against the weeds that bound him.

The snow ceased and the waves settled as we left Draugen behind. The adrenaline faded, and the cold returned. Shivers wracked me.

"Nix!" Del's voice shook from cold. "You've got to conjure...."

Her teeth chattered so hard the words cut off.

"I will." I could no longer see Draugen and the sea was calm, so I turned to my friends, shaking from the cold. They looked like hell—stark white and ragged. I called upon my magic, conjuring space blankets and thermoses of hot coffee. They appeared on the deck in a pile.

"You have quite a skill," Sven said.

"Th-thanks." My teeth chattered as I tugged off my clothes and wrapped one of the space blankets around me. My friends did the same, shaking as they discarded their clothes. The space blanket created warmth, but it was too thin. So I conjured more blankets—big, thick woolen ones.

We wrapped those around us as well, along with hats that I conjured.

"Sure w-wish we could have a fire," Del stuttered.

"Me too." I shook inside the warmth of the blankets.

"No." Sven's voice was firm.

I couldn't blame him. He'd just gotten his boat back—his life. No way he'd risk having a fire on it.

With shaking hands, we drank the thermoses of coffee.

"That was close," Ares said.

"No kidding." I looked between him and Roarke. "Thanks for saving us from the water."

They grinned.

"Anytime," Ares said.

Finally, I was mostly warm enough that I no longer shook uncontrollably. I conjured fresh clothes for each of us, and we tugged them on.

"We'd better get rowing again," Ares said.

"Yeah. Don't want Draugen to shake off the seaweed and catch up," Del said.

I looked at Sven, whose gaze was riveted on the fjord beyond. At least we had our stalwart captain.

"You don't have a spare sail, do you?" I asked.

"I do not."

I called upon my magic, conjuring a sail. It took precious moments to attach it to the spar and hoist it up the mast, but we managed. Once the wind had caught, we each took up an oar and fit it into the oarlock, then sat on a chest and began to row. The exertion sent heat to my muscles. It was good, in a tiring way. As we rowed through the dark night, supplementing the sail power, I focused on my dragon sense, praying that we were close to our destination.

After a while, it tugged hard, toward the shore on our left. I pointed, directing Sven. "That way!"

"There's nothing but cliffs that way!" He squinted toward the mountain that edged the fjord. "No place to land."

My dragon sense was quite clear. "It's over there, I'm sure of it!"

He shrugged and turned the rudder. The boat cut through the water, heading for the cliff. Sven pulled us alongside the towering rock face, and I studied it.

He was right. It was just a straight shot upward, barely any slope at all. But my dragon sense was insistent. I stowed my oar and moved toward the bow, letting my dragon sense guide.

"We're close. I know we are." I squinted at the stone wall. Moonlight gleamed on the rock. A series of strange shadows caught my eye. My heart leapt and I pointed. "There! Stairs carved right into the rock."

Del groaned. "Really? That cliff is thousands of feet tall."

I tilted my head back and looked up. She was right. It was almost inconceivably tall and so steep that it was nearly vertical. The stairs cut into the side, and there was no handrail. My friends rowed slowly as Sven directed the boat toward the stairs.

"Stop!" Sven called.

They stopped rowing, cutting their oars into the water to stop our forward progress. We drifted slowly toward the stairs. Ares handed the amber stone back to Sven, then jumped up and grabbed onto a stone ledge, halting the boat's progress.

"Roarke." I turned to him. "Will you fly up and see if they go all the way to the top?"

He saluted and stowed his oar, then took to the sky, broad wings carrying him upward.

"I could transport us to the top," Ares said.

Sven shook his head. "This is the territory of the elves. If you transport and appear out of nowhere, they will consider it a threat, and you will meet the Dökkálfar, the dark elves. If you take the stairs and make your presence known, you are more likely to meet the Ljósálfar, the light elves."

"Is there a difference?" I asked.

Sven grinned. "You want to meet the light elves."

"Then we'll take the stairs," Ares said.

Roarke returned a moment later, landing softly on the deck. "They do extend all the way up, cut right into the cliffside. They aren't more than two feet wide though. And no railing of any kind, obviously."

My stomach dropped to my feet. I swallowed hard. "This is going to suck."

"Sure is." Del's face was white as she stared up.

"I wish you Godspeed." Sven grinned. "And thank you for awakening me."

"Will you return to your burial place?" I asked.

"Not if I can help it."

"Well, don't lose your boat in that battle, then."

"We'll see." He gazed back over his shoulder, eyes fond.

"Thanks for the ride, Sven." I saluted, then scrambled onto the stairs. Their narrowness made my stomach plunge, and I was only two feet off the water. "We're in for it now."

Del smiled. "I freaking hate stairs like this."

I laughed weakly. The thrill and challenge of it clearly delighted her. Del had always been a danger junkie—jump first, then look.

I turned and began to climb. My friends followed in a single-file line. I was only about twenty feet up when Sven called from down below.

"Be wary, friends! The children of Jörmungand live here."

"What?" I yelled down.

But he was already pulling away, handling his boat so expertly that it cut smoothly through the water. He didn't respond, either because he couldn't hear me or because he didn't want to.

"What is Jörmungand?" Roarke asked.

"The world serpent," Del said. "In Norse mythology, he lives beneath the ocean, so big that he encircles the earth, biting his own tail."

"And his kids live here?" I looked around, searching for snakes. Would they be on the stairs? I shuddered.

"I have no idea what he means," Del said. "I've never read about them."

Del had read about most things, so that wasn't reassuring. While I might be a big reader during my downtime at the shop, Del put me to shame.

"Keep a wary eye out," Ares said.

I did, forcing myself to constantly search the stairs and sea below as we climbed. Sven's boat was but a speck beneath us, sailing off up the fjord.

"I don't think I can look down any longer," Del said.

"Same." The sight was starting to make me queasy. We were already over two hundred feet up, and there were many hundreds more to go. That was a lot of time for the serpents to find us. Could they come from the sea?

"Check behind you, Ares!" I called back to him. "In case the serpents climb out of the water."

"I will."

We continued upward. My thighs burned from the climb and the exhaustion of the day, not to mention my mind. That was exhausted from visions of us falling off the side of this cliff.

The wind cut coldly across my face, chilling my nose until it was numb. I was all but crawling now, clinging to the stone steps and avoiding looking down.

"One thing is for certain," Ares called from the back of the line. "We are definitely going the right way."

"Why do you say that?" I shouted.

"Nothing good ever comes easy!"

I chuckled, my stomach turning as I stole a glance below. We had to be five hundred feet up now. No sign of serpents yet. Maybe Sven had been joking.

We could get that lucky, right?

As soon as I had the thought, I knew I was being an idiot.

*Of course* we wouldn't get that lucky. Not permanently, at least.

We made it another three hundred feet upward, climbing ever more slowly as the exhaustion bit deeper. Victory was near. It would feel like strong, firm ground beneath my feet and no whipping wind or potential plummet to my death.

I could see light at the end of the tunnel when the first shriek rent the night air. My heart leapt into my throat as I plastered myself to the stone steps and searched the stairs above me, then the sky around.

"High on your right!" Roarke shouted.

I looked up, examining the night sky. The Aurora Borealis had appeared, a slight swirl of green against the inky sky. Highlighted against the moon was a winged beast—a serpent.

"Jörmungand's children can *fly*?!" We were screwed.

# CHAPTER EIGHT

"There are more!" Del cried. "Two down below."

My gaze followed her words, seeing two of the beasts hurtling from the depths of the fjord. It was hard to tell how big they were without any scale—*everything* around us was enormous—but they were at least the size of dogs.

Roarke leapt off the stairs, his wings flaring behind him, and flew straight for the closest winged serpent. But there were too many for him to fight alone. I glanced back in time to see Ares draw his shadow sword. Del drew her own blade from the ether.

Heart thundering, I conjured a bow and arrow. It took every ounce of guts that I had to unplaster myself from the stone stairs and kneel. The cold stone bit into my knee, grounding me, tethering me to the earth. I drew back my bowstring, aiming for the closest serpent. When I released the string, my arrow flew straight and true, plunging into the chest of the serpent. The beast bowled backward, flying head over tail toward the water.

Nearby, Roarke tore the head off a serpent with his bare hands, blood spraying. I grimaced. That dude could *fight.*

I conjured another arrow, firing for a serpent headed for Ares. Before the arrow found its mark, I conjured another, firing at a different beast. There were six in the air. Between Roarke and me, we could take them out before Del and Ares had to use their swords. A battle on the stairs was to be avoided at all costs.

I conjured and shot, conjured and shot, taking out three more serpents while Roarke destroyed two. I was aiming for the last when an unholy screech filled the night air. My blood turned to ice in my veins.

That was *way* more than one serpent.

"There!" Del cried, pointing behind us.

I squinted into the dark, catching sight of dozens of serpents flying toward us. They were still a couple hundred meters away, looking no bigger than bats.

"Run!" I screamed.

I dropped my bow, which plunged toward the water below, and raced up the stairs, adrenaline driving me. There would be no winning against that many serpents.

"Come on, Roarke!" Del screamed.

We scrambled up the stairs, Roarke flying at our side. My heart thundered, and my lungs burned, muscles shaking from exhaustion. We still had twenty meters to go.

"They're here!" Ares shouted. "Brace yourselves."

I froze dead in my tracks, turning just my head to look. The serpents were only a dozen yards away, so close that I could make out their brilliant green scales and lacy black wings. Emerald eyes stared ravenously at us, and long fangs dripped with green venom.

*Oh, hell.*

Ares and Del drew their swords from the ether. I conjured a shield, passing it off to Del. "Give it to Ares!"

She handed it down while I conjured another, passing that one to her. By the time she grabbed it, a serpent was upon her, striking with its fangs. She blocked it with the shield. The serpent's head thudded into the metal. Its wings faltered. Del took advantage of the beast's distraction, piercing it with her blade. Below, Ares did the same.

I didn't want to use Laima's blade. I didn't need it for these beasts and was too afraid of dropping it, so I conjured my own sword and shield just before a serpent attacked me. Its sulfurous breath gagged me as I blocked its attack with my shield then struck out with my blade.

It shrieked and plummeted toward the water.

That wasn't so hard!

But the brief flare of hope was suffused by panic at the wall of serpents approaching us through the air. There were even more than before, and there were just so damned *many* of them.

We managed a few steps each before the next wave was upon us. I sliced the neck of one while battering another with my blade, but a third hurtled toward me while my weapons were busy with the other two.

I kicked, nailing the serpent in the face. It shrieked and fell, but another two replaced him. My sword felt heavy in my exhausted arm as I stabbed toward the serpent. I struck him in the chest, but another sank his fangs into my thigh. Pain screamed through me as I yanked my blade from the other serpent's chest and plunged it into the beast that was chewing on my thigh. The monster released its grip with a shriek, and I shook it off my blade.

I turned to face the fjord, searching for my next opponents. Del and Ares were similarly overcome, and Roarke was about to be overpowered as well. Serpents dive-bombed him from all angles, surrounding him.

We were no longer able to climb the stairs—we needed every moment and every ounce of energy to defend against Jörmungand's children.

When four of them charged me, my stomach dropped. I ducked behind my shield and swiped out with my blade, but one of the serpents went straight for my legs, knocking them out from under me. The sword fell from my hand as I lost my footing, going over the edge of the stairs.

I grabbed for the stone ledge, my fingers slipping on the rock, losing contact. My heart almost exploded.

A hand gripped my wrist, giving me just enough support that I could tighten my grip on the stone ledge. Above me, Del was plastered to the stone stairs, holding on to me. Her wide eyes were panicked, the message clear. *We're fucked.*

Serpents screeched as they charged. Ares loomed over Del, fighting them off to give me a chance to scramble onto the stairs, but there were so many. Only his superior speed gave me a shot. Yet I was too weak to haul myself up.

Panic filled my body with a thousand prickles. *Help!* We needed help.

Magic sparked on the air. Jeff appeared next to me, his onyx eyes fixed on me. Behind him, the Pūķi appeared, flaming red in the dark sky.

Immediately, the Pūķi charged the serpents, blowing fire. Jeff, concern so clear in the frantic flutter of his wings, flew down. I lost sight of him, but felt a firm pressure under my butt.

He was trying to push me up! And it worked, just a little. He boosted me enough that I could latch an arm over the stone stairs, then a knee. Del helped me scramble onto firmer ground as Ares fought the serpents who got past the Pūķi's fiery defense.

"Run for it!" Del cried.

I raced up the stairs, my wounded leg aching. The Pūķi held off most of our attackers, blasting their fire at the enemy. I conjured a shield to deflect the rest. They slammed into it as I ran, nipping for my legs. One sank a fang into my calf and I stumbled, hitting my ribs against the stairs. Another bit my thigh.

I clung desperately as pain surged through me, determined not to fall again, then clambered up and continued. We were so close! Just five more stairs.

I lunged for solid ground, dragging myself up. Del followed, then Ares, all of us collapsing on the snow.

Immediately, Del crawled around and screamed, "Roarke!"

He hurtled out of the night sky, headed straight for us. Blood poured from dozens of bite wounds. The serpents followed him, their green eyes ravenous.

Jeff fluttered at my side, concerned eyes watching the scene.

My stomach lurched. Though we were on solid ground, there were still the monsters to contend with. And there were dozens.

I tried to ignore the pain coursing through me as I staggered to my feet, shield raised. I conjured another sword, bracing myself for impact.

The horde of serpents was nearly upon us, only twenty feet away. Their fangs gleamed in the moonlight. I was nearly numb with terror, an animal driven by instinct to live.

Roarke hurtled to the ground next to us, skidding on the snow. He left a trail of bloody white. The serpents that had pursued him stopped dead in their tracks, wings holding them aloft in a line just ten feet from us. They hissed, their frustration clear, then spun and flew away, plummeting down to the water below.

I stumbled back, panting. Adrenaline made my head woozy.

"Why did they stop?" Ares asked. "They're not afraid of us."

Del rushed toward Roarke, who lay in the snow. I turned to face Ares, briefly catching sight of his blood-covered body before my gaze fell upon a line of mounted warriors. There were six of them, each dressed in pale blue with white hair and eyes.

*Oh, crap.*

*These* were the people who had scared Jörmungand's children.

"Turn around, Ares."

He spun, sword raised. Immediately, he lowered his blade. Del helped Roarke to his feet.

Two of the mounted figures rode forward. A man and a woman, each wearing identical uniforms. Theirs were fancier than the others, tunics shot through with silver thread that matched their long hair. Though their eyes were entirely whited out, it was clear that they stared at us. Pointed ears peeked through their hair.

The elves.

*Please be the light elves.*

"Vampire, why did you not transport to the top?" the woman asked.

Ares stepped forward, his limp minimized, no doubt to show no weakness. "We were told it would be construed as an attack, and in that event, we would meet the dark elves. I have heard of the dark elves. I prefer to meet Jörmungand's children."

The elves smiled, their teeth white and perfect. Though they were beautiful, it was a terrifying smile. Their magic rolled off of them in waves, crushingly powerful. We were outmanned here, no question.

"Wise choice," the woman said. "I am Alva. The commander of this regiment. You are on our land. What do you seek here?"

"Answers," I said. "Just answers."

"How can we trust you?"

*Uhh.*

Jeff chose that moment to flutter out from behind my back, where he'd been hiding. My little dragon was brave, but he knew how to choose his battles.

Alva's gaze landed on Jeff and widened. A flash of red caught my eye. The Pūķi had joined us. Alva's white brows rose even higher. "You have dragons."

"I do. Sort of. They're made more of magic than of flesh and bone, but they are dragons. Though not in the ancient sense."

A smile tugged at Alva's lips. "I can see that. They are far too small. But it is an accepted truth that dragons only congregate with the worthy. As you have *three* of them, we will permit you entrance to our land."

I nearly sagged with relief. Unfortunately, fear had been the only thing keeping me upright. I'd been going on nothing but adrenaline and terror for the last several hours.

Ares held out a hand. I grabbed it, supporting myself with one arm and the very last of my strength. I could have kissed him for not coming over and swooping me up. I was the leader of our merry little band, and he knew as well as I how important it was to show strength. He gave me only what I needed to save myself from face-planting in the snow.

"And a healer," the male elf said. "You need a healer. The venom of Jörmungand's children is toxic."

"Toxic?" Del's voice was frantic. She supported Roarke, who was riddled with so many puncture wounds that he looked like an old pincushion. She didn't look much better, having taken several hits while trying to drag me up onto the stairs after I'd fallen. They were probably both leaning against each other.

"Curable." The elf nodded at Roarke. "Even for him. But it is best if we start now."

"Yes." Del nodded frantically.

"Follow us." Alva turned her horse.

Ares looked down at me. "I'm going to help Roarke. I don't think he can walk. Can you manage?"

I nodded. Jeff came to fly under my arm. I put a hand on his back, drawing a bit of strength from him. It flowed into my muscles, warm and wonderful. "Thanks, pal."

Ares took Roarke from Del, wrapping Roarke's arm around his own shoulders and helping him limp toward the retreating elves. Del staggered toward me, hardly able to walk. I reached out for her, wrapping an arm around her waist. We lurched after Roarke and Ares. Jeff gave me just enough strength to walk, but the snow made it hard going.

When we reached a massive tree in the middle of a clearing, my jaw dropped. It was bigger than a redwood, with wooden stairs built in a spiral all around. High above, lights glittered in the trees.

"We live above," Alva said.

"More stairs?" Del sounded like she was going to cry. I couldn't blame her.

I sucked in a shuddery breath and moved toward the stairs. As soon as I stepped onto the first one, warmth flowed through me. The air changed, just slightly. Warmer and full of magic.

I looked at Alva. "What is that?"

"Our realm. This is a gateway to our world. We defend this outpost. But the tree is able to take some of the magic from Álfheimr, our homeland."

"Wow." It made me feel slightly stronger, enough so I could make it to the top. Maybe.

Alva nodded. "Wow is correct."

We climbed the stairs that spiraled around the tree. Even Roarke could get himself up with the help of the magic, though his wounds continued to weep blood and green poison. By the time I reached the main building high in the branches, I was super ready to be done with today.

The stairs led into a main room that was built entirely of pale white wood. It was octagonal shaped, with large windows looking out to the branches beyond. Skylights revealed the Aurora Borealis, which was brightening as the night went on, reds and purples being added to the green. Sparkling golden lights glittered in the ceiling—fairy lights. Literally. Even my pain couldn't keep me from chuckling quietly at the bad pun.

There was little furniture in the space, just an open fire pit surrounded by plush blue cushions.

We all stripped off our heavy jackets and hung them on hooks near the door. Jeff gave me one last look and disappeared. I assumed he went back to my trove, but I couldn't say for certain.

"These elves really have a thing for blue," Del whispered

"I was just thinking that." I kept my voice low.

Most of the elves went through a doorway on the other side

of the room. Alva turned to us and gestured to the cushions. "You may have a seat. I will bring a healer and some food."

Gratefully, I collapsed onto a plush cushion. Ares and Del sat next to me, with Roarke nearly keeling over on a cushion next to Del.

"Are you okay, Roarke?" I asked.

"Fine," he slurred.

"Fighting in the air amongst Jörmungand's children was brave," Ares said.

I looked at him, surprised to see how much more blood had seeped from wounds beneath his clothes. He'd probably received them while defending Del and me as she'd tried to haul me back up onto the stairs.

I frowned at Ares. "You really got it, too."

He shrugged. "None of us escaped unharmed."

That was the truth.

A moment later, Alva returned with a healer. The newest elf was older, her face lined and her posture stooped.

"This is Astrid," Alva said. "She is very talented."

I nodded. "Thank you for coming."

"Will you see to Roarke first?" Del asked.

Astrid's white eyes traveled to Roarke and she nodded. "That would be for the best." Her voice reminded me of a birdsong.

She sat at Roarke's side. She had no medical instruments, so I assumed it would be a magical sort of healing. When she hovered her hands over Roarke's body, blue light glowed from her palms. He winced as green venom seeped from his wounds, brilliant beneath the fairy lights.

Slowly he relaxed. The most obvious of his wounds closed up. After five minutes, he was sitting straighter, his gaze brighter.

"Thank you." He nodded to Astrid.

"Hmmm." She turned to Ares. "You next."

They were the worst off by far. Astrid was quicker with Ares, and quicker yet with Del. I'd been lucky with only a few puncture wounds, possibly because of my positioning on the steps.

When Astrid hovered her hands over me, warmth flowed from her palm. My wounds burned fiercely as the poison leached from my flesh, but comfort came when the poison was gone and Astrid's magic closed the tears.

"That's amazing, thank you," I said.

"Hmmm." She gave a small smile and stood, then left the room.

"She doesn't speak much, does she?" I asked Alva.

"Not to you, no. Many of our kind are insular. She doesn't mind helping you, but she is thousands of years old. She can't imagine you'd have anything new to tell her."

I chuckled. "Fair enough."

Three elves entered the room, each carrying a tray laden with glasses and food. The savory smell of spices hit my nose, and my mouth watered. Though I was so exhausted that my body felt like a pile of spaghetti, my stomach grumbled. I could find the energy to eat.

Alva took a seat across from us, joined by the male elf that had ordered the healer. She gestured to him. "This is Eirik."

I nodded hello as other elves set the food on a nearby table, then served us each a plate of food and a goblet of amber liquid.

"Thank you," we all spoke at the same time, each of us clearly grateful for the sustenance.

I chowed down, trying not to be a pig about it but so famished that I probably looked pretty desperate. Everything on my plate was some form of vegetable—none of which I recognized—but it was all delicious.

With the worst of my hunger sated, I looked up at Alva. "Thank you again for your assistance."

She nodded. "It is rare that someone visits our land. It is difficult to reach."

"That's an understatement," Ares said.

"Yes, well, you made it to the top. Clearly your goal is important to you. Which direction are you headed?"

"Northwest." At least, that was where my dragon sense was currently pulling me.

Alva frowned. "That will be difficult. You've reached a region where supernaturals reign supreme in Norway. As I'm sure you know, we don't do anything in half measures here."

"I can see that." Jörmungand's children had made it very clear.

"We will send a scout with you to the border of our land, along with reindeer for you to ride. There are some rune stones at the border that will help you cross the next part of your journey."

"How so?" Ares asked.

"Ask them your questions, and they will give you answers. There are parts of our land upon which you must not tread. It will become more clear tomorrow."

I hoped so, because that was about as clear as mud. "Thank you for the help."

"It is the least we can do." Alva's gaze zeroed in on me. "Your dragon makes it clear that you are meant to do something great. Dragons would not accompany the unworthy."

I just hoped I could live up to Jeff's faith in me, then.

Alva rose and gestured to a door to the left. "There are sleep quarters there for you, along with a bath. We will see you in the morning."

She and Eirik departed, leaving us alone.

"Well, this has been some good luck," Del said.

"Yeah. I don't know if we'd have survived otherwise," I said.

"We'd have managed," Ares said. "Though barely."

I sipped the wine. The most divine taste exploded over my tongue. It was as delicious as Laima's Ambrosia. Maybe even better.

"This is amazing." I held up the glass.

Ares's gaze sharpened. "Do not drink too much. It is elven

wine. Stronger stuff than we mere mortals can tolerate. Be wary here."

He was right. Though warm and comforting, it was dangerous. I nodded as I sipped again, my head buzzing with pleasure. I just felt *happy*. I sipped again.

Ares reached out for the glass, taking it from me. "Be wary. The elves help us and we can trust them, but not all in their world is made for us. We are in the realm of the gods here, a place with more magic than we've ever known. It is dangerous because of that."

I was getting serious déjà vu. First the tricky goddesses and their Ambrosia, and now the elves with their wine. "You're right. We need to keep our wits about us." I stood. "I'm ready for a bath and bed."

Everyone else stood, and we went into the bedroom. It was a simple room, with four long, plush cushions on the floor for sleeping and two doors leading out of the room.

I peeked my head into both, finding a fabulous shower room in one and a steam bath in the other. Both had ceilings of glass.

"How do they handle plumbing?" Del asked.

"Magic?" I couldn't imagine running pipes up into the tree. For one, it was alive, so you couldn't run them through the trunk. And we hadn't seen them when we'd climbed the stairs.

"Nix and Del, you can go first," Ares said.

"Thanks." I hurried into the shower room with Del.

The room was built of the same pale wood, but half was tiled with sparkling beige stones. Small waterfalls poured from three spouts against the wall. Quickly, I stripped off my clothes and ducked under one of the showers. The water was warm, and the pressure felt like a massage against my aching shoulders.

Del did the same, ducking under her own waterfall.

"This is amazing," I murmured.

"No kidding." She paused. "So, it's really getting serious between you and Ares, huh?"

"Yeah, kinda. I really like him. A lot. And Laima has confirmed that it's not a product of the blood bond. That we're fated."

Del spit out water. "Whoa, fated? That's really a thing?"

"For vampires, I guess. And me, apparently."

"Wow. How do you feel about that?"

"Well, I'm not a big fan of fate deciding things for me. But I like Ares. So maybe fate's not so far off."

"Well, I like him. He hasn't taken his eyes off you the whole time we've been out here."

My heart warmed. I finished showering, scrubbing the rest of the blood and poison from my skin, then grabbed one of the fluffy towels from a shelf by the window. It wasn't terrycloth like a human towel, which was no surprise. I couldn't imagine an elf in Bed, Bath, and Beyond. The fabric was silky and absorbent. There were silk PJs on the shelf as well.

"Toss me a pair of those, will you?" Del asked.

I threw her a pair—of course they were light blue—and pulled on my own. We traded places with the guys, who looked like hell. They'd obviously chosen to try out the steam room, and streaks of sweat cut through the blood on their arms. I raised my brow at Ares.

"It was a mistake." He grinned. "But it looked nice, so we tried it."

I laughed and pointed to the shower. "Get in there."

Del and I settled onto the cushions on the floor. I moaned as it enveloped me, cloud-like softness welcoming me into its embrace. I pulled the silken blanket—blue, of course—over me and stared at the glass ceiling above. Swirls of color painted the night sky.

"Beautiful, isn't it?" I yawned.

If Del responded, I didn't hear it. Sleep had never claimed me so fast in my whole life.

# CHAPTER NINE

The next morning, after a breakfast of more vegetables and a divine bread that was soft as a cloud, we descended the stairs from the elven fortress. I felt a thousand times better after food and sleep. The elves had even given us winter clothes to wear, since ours had been soaked in blood and venom. Of course they were blue, but it'd saved me from having to conjure any, so I was at full strength and ready to rock.

The sun was just starting to peek over the horizon, spreading a pink glow across the snow. Since it was winter in Norway, that didn't mean it was particularly warm, however. By my estimate, it was slightly after nine.

At the base of the tree, five reindeer waited. They were bigger than normal reindeer, their backs almost level with my head. They wore cream-colored saddles with blue embellishments.

Alva gestured to the animals. "Your rides."

"Thank you." It took me a few tries to climb onto the back of the reindeer closest to me. Twice, it turned around to look at me, its eyes clearly saying, "You're new at this, aren't you?"

"Give me a break, Rudolph," I muttered.

Ares chuckled from behind me, then gripped my waist and lifted me enough so that I could climb on.

"Thanks." I smiled at him.

"Anytime." He leapt onto his own mount, looking like he'd been born in the reindeer saddle.

Eirik mounted his reindeer in one smooth move and directed the beast to stand in front of us. "I'll lead you through the forest. Follow my directions, and we'll be fine."

I saluted. He frowned at me.

Whoops.

"May fate be with you," Alva said.

"Thank you for the help." I waved goodbye and directed my mount after Eirik.

We trailed in a line after him, Ares behind me, with Del and Roarke following him. Trees rose tall around us as we rode over the sparkling snow. The elves' winter clothing was light, but warm. If only the rest of our journey could be this comfortable.

We rode for over an hour in peaceful silence. The sun crept higher in the sky. I was just about lulled into complacency when Eirik stopped his mount abruptly and held out a hand. He cocked his head, listening.

I did the same, but heard nothing.

"Go!" he shouted, spurring on his mount.

*Crap!* I nudged my reindeer with my heels. The beast set off, galloping across the snow. I clung for dear life, bouncing in the saddle.

"Avoid the wisps!" Eirik shouted.

Wisps? I looked around, frantic to see the threat. The forest looked the same—tall trees and glittering snow. Except now there were hazy white ghosts zipping through the air. They were small and formless, glowing with a white light.

Wisps, definitely. I had no idea what they did, but if Eirik was riding like mad, I was going to follow.

One of the wisps zipped closer to me, headed straight for my mount. I pulled the reins left, dodging by an inch. Snow kicked up from the reindeer's heels as we galloped after Eirik. Another wisp came from the right. We veered away, narrowly avoiding that one, too.

We'd made it another twenty meters when two wisps came at the same time, hurtling through the air. I dodged one, but the other hit my mount square in the neck. The reindeer shrieked and bucked, going up on his hind legs.

I clung to his back, but he bucked again. I lost my grip, flying off into the snow. The air whooshed out of me as I slammed against the ground.

"Up!" Eirik shouted.

Panting, I scrambled up. Ares was galloping right for me, arm outstretched. I reached for him, grabbing his arm as he swung me up onto the saddle in front of him. My heart soared. It was a move worthy of a movie.

I clung to his reindeer's neck as we raced after Eirik. My reindeer was going wild in the distance, racing through the trees and chasing the wisps.

Ares directed us around more of the shooting white lights, barely escaping them time and again. By the time Eirik slowed his reindeer, I was panting from the exertion of holding on to the wildly galloping reindeer.

"What were those things?" I asked.

Eirik gazed back into the distance, no doubt at the reindeer we'd lost. "Wisps possess an animal, turning it feral. That reindeer is one with the forest, now."

"People, too?" I asked.

Eirik nodded. "We're lucky we weren't hit. It's impossible to predict where the wisps will travel."

Del slumped over her mount, panting. "Whoever said riding isn't a workout is an idiot."

I laughed, still breathless.

The barest smile tugged at the lips of the stoic elf. He turned his reindeer. "Come, we must go on."

We followed him through the forest, silent and alert for more wisps. I leaned back against Ares, absorbing his warmth as we rode. The sun rose higher in the sky as the day progressed.

Finally, Eirik pointed ahead. "The stones are there."

I squinted across the bright snow. There were three standing stones, each enormous. As we neared, I realized that they were at least fifty feet tall. Bigger even than the stones at Stonehenge.

Eirik led us right up to the base of the largest one. There were no runes carved upon its surface.

"Where are the runes?" I asked.

"You must ask it your question." He paused, face grave. "Choose wisely."

"Any question, huh?"

"Yes. And remember—you face great dangers ahead."

"What kind?"

He shrugged. "That depends. Your question may help you with that."

I looked back at my friends. Del and Roarke directed their mounts up to stand next to me.

"What do you guys think? My Seeker sense is already leading us to our answers." Though I was pretty sure that Eirik didn't give a damn if I was a FireSoul, I was careful to use my usual lie. "But it doesn't take into account the dangers ahead."

"Isn't that the truth. If it was any good at avoiding danger, we'd have taken a different route."

"So we should ask it the safest way to get to where we're going," Ares asked.

"Yep. Because getting killed on the way would be a bummer," I said.

Roarke nodded. "Agreed."

I turned to the rune stones. "We are headed west, toward a

mountain." It was all I knew, and I hoped it was enough. "What dangers face us, and how can we avoid them?"

Magic sparked on the air as the stone glowed with faint light. Runes carved themselves into the stone, unreadable but amazing all the same.

Eirik directed his mount to the stone, gazing up at the writing. "You must head south, avoid the Jötunn. Do not let them find you as you follow the white hare to the mountain beyond. Do not deviate from the hare's path."

"Jötunn are giants, aren't they?" Del asked.

"They are. Like us, they have a section of earthly land in this forest. They like to hunt there. They would not be opposed to eating you." His brows lowered. "Should they find you, you will not win. The giants can defeat even us. Avoid their notice. Though one tip—their vision is not good."

"Can we transport through this area?" Ares asked.

"You can, but only if you want to risk getting lost. This is the gods' land now. Like us, they do not appreciate people appearing out of the blue."

Ares nodded. "Thank you for your help."

He inclined his head. "Fate be with you. And the reindeer must come with me."

Dang. I climbed down off the reindeer and patted his head, feeling guilty about my reindeer that'd gone feral. "The reindeer that ran off. Will he be okay?"

Eirik nodded. "He is one with the forest now. He'll be happy."

Whew. Eirik departed, the reindeer following along docile.

I turned to my friends. "How about some snowshoes?"

"Good idea." Del pulled her foot out of the snow, which reached above her ankle.

I conjured snowshoes and handed them off to the group, then sat and strapped mine onto my boots. When I stood, it was much easier to walk. We set off through the forest, going south around the Jötunn's territory.

We walked in silence, keeping our ears perked for any kind of noise that might indicate a giant was nearby. Birds twittered in the trees, snowy white things that looked like snowballs perched on the branches. As we walked, the sun crept across the sky. At best, we only had a few hours left of daylight.

"I'm not sure how much farther west we should go," I said. "It's easy to follow my sense directly, but deviating is difficult."

Ares pointed ahead of us. "What about that?"

I looked, catching sight of a white hare waiting patiently for us. "Our guide."

The animal didn't speak—though it wouldn't have surprised me if it did—but it watched us until we'd all looked at it, then turned and hopped off through the forest. We followed, hurrying after the small animal.

A half hour later, thunder shook the air. I looked up. "There are no clouds."

"Shh." Ares held a finger to his lips.

I stiffened, looking around. Beneath me, the ground trembled. If I'd had a cup of water, ripples would be forming on the surface.

"Giants," Ares mouthed.

I spun, searching the terrain. There was nowhere to hide, just tall trees and endless snow. But the ground shook harder. The thunder boomed again, and I realized it was a shout, not thunder.

"We have to hide," Del whispered.

She was right. We couldn't outrun him. And I believed Eirik when he'd said we could not fight him. But where to hide?

"His vision is bad," Ares whispered.

That was it. Just like a T-Rex. I gestured for them to follow me to the base of a large tree. I lay down and they followed, all of us pressed up against each other. I conjured a big white tarp and laid it on top of us, then whispered to Del, "Can you cover us with snow?"

Del nodded, her magic flaring, and used her ice power to create a thin layer of snow that weighted our blanket down.

My heart thundered as we waited, our breath held. Could the giant hear my heartbeat? It was so loud it sounded like a beating drum. The ground shook with every footfall. Ares squeezed my hand.

I felt like that kid in *Jurassic Park*, frozen and terrified, waiting to see if the T-Rex would spot him moving.

Soon, the footsteps were so close that it felt like my organs were vibrating.

*Please don't step on us.*

I prayed that he wouldn't come so close to the base of the tree, but would stick to the open snow where it was easier to walk.

Loud, low voices sounded, booming like foghorns.

Two giants, talking. But I couldn't understand them.

I held stiff as a board, trying not to breathe loudly as my mind raced with ideas about what would happen if we were discovered. Eaten? Stepped upon? Kept as pets for giants?

I shivered.

The giants stepped closer, their footfalls shaking the ground. Panic swelled in my chest. They were too close! And getting closer.

Shit, shit, shit.

This wasn't going to work.

Frantic, my mind scrambled for ideas. Maybe the trees could help us. But how? I envisioned them, tall and covered in thick pine needles and large pinecones.

I reached out to the forest, trying to feel the trees' life signatures. I'd never done anything quite like this, but it was our last shot. Slowly, they came online, appearing out of the darkness of my mind.

I crossed my fingers as I called out to a tree that was about fifty meters away. It was covered heavily in pine cones—how I knew that, I had no idea. Maybe because pinecones were new life and I could sense that? Whatever. I wasn't going to look gift magic in the mouth. I reached for the tree's life magic, focusing on the pinecones and commanding them to fly off the tree towards us, hoping to hit the giants who were nearby.

A tense moment passed, then two. Finally, the tree heeded my commands, hurling its pinecones at the Jötunn. One of them roared, a sound of surprise that shook the snow around us. I held my breath as I waited to see what they would do. Their footsteps thundered away as I'd hope, no doubt in search of the assailant. We lay in silence for a few minutes, listening to the Jötunn retreat.

"I think we're safe," Ares whispered.

I nodded, then tugged down on the tarp to peek out. Cold snow sneaked beneath it, chilling my skin. I shivered and popped my head out of the snow. Massive footprints led away from us, and in the distance I could see enormous figures running in the other direction, perhaps thinking that they pursued their attackers.

When they disappeared, I pulled the tarp away. "We're good."

Del stood and shook the snow from her head. "What the heck happened?"

"I asked a tree to chuck some pinecones at them." The pinecones in question were scattered all over the ground. "Looks like it worked."

"Amazing." Del shook her head.

"Quick thinking," Ares said. "Did you know you could do that."

"Nope. Just figuring it out as I go along." I grinned. "Pretty cool though."

"More than cool." Ares turned to inspect the forest, his gaze landing on the white hare that waited in the distance, watching us quietly. "Let's go."

We set off through the forest, following the hare. We saw no more giants, finally reaching a mountain that rose steeply into the sky. The hare gave us one last look, then hopped away.

"Looks like we're in for a hike," I said. "But we're close. I can feel it."

"We've got two hours till dark," Ares said.

"I think we can do it." The mountain was high, but not that high. The incline would be a problem though. My stomach grumbled. "Let's eat quickly, then get a move on."

We pulled off the packs the elves had given us and chowed down on the sandwiches inside. Warmth and strength flowed through me.

Bolstered, we started to climb, quickly discarding our snowshoes. I used a bit of my destroyer magic to make them disappear, then stepped back and dusted off my hands. "There, no littering."

"You're getting good at that."

"Practice makes perfect. Though it still feels kinda gross to use that magic." The nice warmth the food had put in my belly had been replaced with a light queasiness. No doubt using that magic would always make me feel kinda crappy.

I conjured crampons, and we strapped them on. The metal spikes made it easier to ascend the mountain, and soon we were panting with exertion. My chest heaved as I put one foot in front of the other, determined to reach the top before nightfall. We went in a line, Ares leading the way. The sun was on the far side of the sky now, sinking toward the horizon.

"An hour till dark," Ares said.

I looked up, barely able to see the peak at the top through the white clouds that drifted around it. It looked like Mount Olympus. *Nope, wrong mythology.* That one was way farther south and way less cold.

I sucked in a ragged breath and quickened my pace, trying to keep up with Ares. As we neared the top, magic sparked on the air. My heartbeat thudded in my ears.

Were the dragons here? I was leading us toward answers, and that was all I knew. Maybe the dragons were actually here.

"Look." Ares pointed ahead.

I squinted into the distance. We were basically at the top, and about a hundred meters away sat a dark, spired building. I hurried toward it, getting a better look as we neared.

The building was a moderate size, made of very dark wood with steep, multi-level roofs that terminated at a delicate spire that reached into the clouds. Intricate carvings covered the walls. It was gorgeous.

"It's a stave church," Del said. "Those are a thousand years old."

"And they're still standing?" I asked.

She nodded. "There are twenty-eight known stave churches in Norway, all of them built around 1000 AD."

"I'd bet this one makes twenty-nine," Ares said.

"Yeah," Del said. "This one isn't normal. It has three doors, for one."

Each was surrounded by carved trim, so intricate and delicate that it boggled the mind.

"Let's approach." I stepped forward slowly, walking quietly toward the door. When I neared the building, I bent over and removed my crampons so that the metal spikes wouldn't hurt the wooden floor.

"Which door?" Ares asked.

"Middle." I followed my dragon sense to that door, opening it slowly to reveal the dim interior of the church. The wood was dark in here as well, no bright paintings or stained glass like you'd find in other churches. It was beautiful all the same, with its ornate wooden carvings and the history steeped in the walls.

Magic filled the space, a signature I'd never encountered before. It was neither sound, smell, taste, sight, nor physical feeling. But rather a sense of ancientness and gravity. Though I often felt that at historical sites, this was something more.

I entered the dimly lit interior, followed by my friends. Ares used his magic to illuminate the room. The glow lit the space, revealing the carved statue of a woman in the middle. She looked fierce, her body armored and her hands clutching a sword that stood in front of her, tip pointing toward the ground.

"That's gotta be important," Del said.

"Yep." I walked slowly toward the statue, Del at my side. Ares and Roarke followed behind, giving us space.

The woman gazed ahead, her wooden expression impassive. Her shield bore a carved handprint.

Del reached up and laid her hand against it. Nothing happened. She withdrew. "You try."

I touched the handprint, laying my palm flat against the wood. Magic sparked up my arm, electricity that set me alive. The wood beneath my palm vibrated. Gasping, I jerked my hand away and stepped back.

Ares and Roarke stepped forward as if to defend us, but I threw out my arm to stop them.

A ghost stepped out of the statue, semi-transparent but in full color. A woman. Wings flared off her back, and she relaxed her arm to hold her sword at her side. The light from Ares's palms glowed off her golden hair and silver armor.

*Hang on...*

Wings, armor, sword, super warrior woman. Was she a Valkyrie?

# CHAPTER TEN

The Valkyrie's gaze landed on me.

"Finally, you have arrived." Power resonated in her voice.

I glanced at my friends, which was dumb, because obviously she was speaking to me. But it was entirely disconcerting to have that much power focused solely in my direction. "Yes. I'm seeking answers about how to save the dragons from Drakon."

She smiled and inclined her head. "You have come to the correct place. I am Hildr. I have been waiting to deliver my message to you for a thousand years."

"*Wow.*" Immediately, I wanted to take back the inane statement. But really. *Wow.*

"Wow, indeed." Hildr smiled. "To save the dragons, you must first understand their true nature. Do you think that you do?"

"No. Not even close."

"But you are a FireSoul."

"I know. But I don't know how I became one or what it means." None of the FireSouls that I'd ever met understood. All of the other magical powers were inherited traits. Not being a FireSoul. But no one knew why. "And all I know about dragons is that they are fierce, huge warriors."

Hildr looked at my friends. "Do you know anything about the nature of dragons?"

They, too, shook their heads.

She smiled, almost sad. "How the world has changed. We understood, in my time. But it has been a thousand years. I have watched the world from Valhalla. Watched as the dragons went underground and the world forgot them. Now their legend is lost to time. They've become mythical beasts, but their true nature— the most important thing about them—is buried in the mists of the past. But it is more disappointing than I realized."

I wanted to apologize, but I couldn't speak for the world. "What happened to them?"

"*Who* happened to them, is what you should ask. And why." Her gaze turned distant. "Long ago, dragons flew freely. Humans could not see them, for they were made of pure magic, but supernaturals could. There were many. Dozens, all over the world, flying through the sky, as big as the great hall at Valhalla. Their magic covered the world. It fueled the rest of the supernaturals, giving us our strength."

"What do you mean?"

Her voice lowered, carrying power with it. "'For all the magic of the world is housed within the dragons.'" She blinked, as if coming out of a trance. "That was part of the prophecy that you learned, but it had been lost long ago."

"Are you saying that all supernaturals' magic comes from dragons?" Ares asked.

"I am. Not just the magic of FireSouls, but the magic of mages, weres, vampires, and the fae. *Everything* came from the dragons. They are the source of our magic, sharing it with us so that we may be more than human."

"How do we not know that?" That was *huge*. "Most people think that magic is innate. It exists, just like hydrogen or gold."

"We Valkyrie have hidden that information. It is too dangerous to be in the hands of the greedy. As our story will now prove. A thousand years ago, during my time, a great evil rose. A man, an ancient immortal who wanted all of the world's magic for himself."

I shivered. "Drakon. He really is ancient."

"Yes. He hunted the dragons for centuries, learning about them and creating his plan. Six hundred years ago, after much practice, his power came to full strength. He found a way to steal the magic from the dragons. And he succeeded, in part, killing many of them and taking their power."

*Bastard.* "That's why he looks like a shadow dragon."

"Yes. He was so successful that it became clear he would stamp out all the dragons in the world. And if he succeeded in that, then every supernatural on Earth would lose their power, because Drakon would not share."

"Oh, *shit.*" Losing your magic was almost a fate worse than death. It felt like someone had stolen your soul. Suddenly, there was so much more at stake. Not just the dragons, but the soul of every supernatural on Earth. "What happened?"

"The Valkyries—my sisters and I—put a spell on the last living dragons, hiding them. Buying them time to recoup their strength. Dragons are a communal society, you see. With so many of their brethren dead, they were weaker. Too weak to fight Drakon and recover what he had stolen from them."

"The magic of their brethren?"

"Yes. Though their kin were gone, they could not let Drakon keep their magic. However, they were too weak to fight. So the Valkyrie hid them, concealing them with a spell while they slept. But before they went to their slumber, the dragons each imparted a piece of their soul to special individuals throughout the world. They chose the bravest and the most honorable. It was their way of keeping their magic alive and active."

"Oh my gosh—" My jaw dropped. I snapped it shut. "Do you mean us? Is that how FireSouls were created?"

"Yes. The FireSouls keep the dragons' spirits alive—their

118

magic alive—while they sleep. They are the dragons' tether to the world."

"Then if all the FireSouls die, so do the dragons," I said.

"Yes. That is why there are many of you, though not as many as there once were. But three of you are the most important."

"The Triumvirate."

"Yes."

"The dragons have been gone almost five hundred years. But I'm a fraction that old. How did they give me their soul hundreds of years after they went to sleep?"

"You are reincarnated, as all FireSouls are. Your soul has been joined to a dragon's for hundreds of years."

My legs weakened. Wow. I'd had no idea I was a reincarnate. They were rare. "So Drakon is seeking the last of the dragons to steal their power."

"Yes. It's taken him centuries to track them down and find them. And to find how to take the last of their power. The remaining three dragons are the strongest that ever lived. He needed time to find them."

I nodded, swallowing hard. "How do I save them?"

"You must stop him from stealing their power. He is not a FireSoul who can steal magic, so he must use a complex spell. If it is the same one that he used before—which it likely is—then it is the Encapsulata Theiva curse. It takes great strength and great sacrifice."

"How does it work?" I asked.

"It's a combination spell. One that freezes the victims before sucking out their magic. It appears as a dome of dark smoke. Once trapped by this smoke, you cannot move."

Recognition tugged at me. *Oh no.*

"It is all powered by a magical power source and conduit. This is what allows him to take the magic for his own. But one must have enormous power to put this plan into motion, as well as have the power source and conduit."

"What do you mean by power source and conduit?" Ares asked.

"There are many things that could work. Ancient artifacts imbued with great magic, for one. You will have to find what he is using to understand. Oftentimes, it's hidden near the magical dome that freezes the victims. It has to be, to funnel the power."

*Magical dome that freezes the victims.* Understanding dawned, dark and horrible in my mind. "He's stealing the magic from the people of Elesius."

Everyone's head turned toward me.

"What do you mean?" Del asked.

My heart thundered in my ears, blood rushing through my veins. "That's what he's doing to my village. He isn't just freezing them. It's not just a ploy to catch us. It's to take their magic."

I dragged in a ragged breath, so appalled I almost couldn't fathom it. Losing ones magic was like losing one's soul. It was enough that *I* had taken all the plant magic. This spell would steal the magic of the individuals as well, leaving them as half the people they had once been. It would leave a gaping hole that would feel like part of their soul had been stolen.

"This is your home village?" Hildr asked.

I nodded. "Two days ago, I went to visit and found a smoky black dome like the one you are speaking of. I think he's doing exactly what you say."

"That is very possible. And he may be trying to weaken you. Your magic comes from Elesius. If he steals it all, then you would be left with so much less."

"I thought I'd already taken all the magic from Elesius. The plants there are so dead."

Hildr shook her head. "The whole place is tied to you. If he succeeds, it will hurt you as well."

I scowled. "That bastard is efficient."

"And intelligent. And evil. You must defeat him. You and Drakon were meant to clash. You are the last defense for the dragons, but you are also the tool by which they can be destroyed."

"How will he use us to destroy the dragons?" I asked.

"It is related to stealing their power, but the details...I do not know. Nor do I know exactly how you are meant to save them other than keeping him from stealing their power. But you have a weapon to help you."

"I do." I withdrew the sword from the sheath at my back. "It was given to me by Laima, the Latvian goddess of faith."

A smile stretched across Hildr's face. "I know Laima well. It's been a millennia since we've spoken, but we were friends once." She inspected my blade with keen eyes. "You will use that to destroy the threat to your village. It is a cancer that must be destroyed from the inside, and only that blade can manage the task."

"What do you mean, a cancer from inside?"

"Only that. You will know when you see it."

Oh, man. That was clear as mud. "Is there anything else that you can tell us? Where are the dragons?"

"They are resting in the tallest mountain in Norway. High above the clouds and deep below the magma."

"What does that mean?"

"That is all that I can share. Fate be with you, Phoenix Knight. We are depending upon you. What the Valkyries started, you must finish."

*No pressure.* My mind raced for more questions. But the air shimmered and Hildr disappeared, leaving me with no one to ask.

～

We had to climb down the mountain in the dark because Ares's transportation magic wouldn't work near the ancient stave church. No wonder—I couldn't imagine the Valkyries wanting people to pop out of nowhere with no warning. I just hoped we wouldn't have to go all the way back to the entrance of the fjord. The glow from Ares's hands lit the way down, gleaming on the snow. Wind whipped past us, howling in the dark. It was an eerie trek, and I sighed with relief when we reached the bottom.

I shivered and turned to Ares. "Will your magic work here?"

"I think so." He held out his hand, and I took it.

"I'll wait with Roarke," Del said.

Ares nodded, then called upon his magic. The ether sucked us in, and gratitude welled in me. Thank fates we didn't have to make our way back across this treacherous land.

The afternoon sun shined high overhead when we reached Magic's Bend. Though there was a winter bite in the air, it was nothing compared to the whistling cold of the Norwegian winter. It was nearly balmy here.

I sagged, relieved to be home. "Thanks for the ride."

"Anytime." He grinned. "Be right back."

"I'll meet you at P & P."

He disappeared and I walked down the street toward P & P, hoping my favorite chair would be empty. The golden warmth of the cafe welcomed me as I pushed open the door and stepped inside. Music played on the speakers. Ghoston Road, I thought Connor had once called it. As usual, my chair was empty. I suspected that Connor or Claire had enchanted it. They were cool like that.

Connor looked up from behind the counter and grinned. "Any luck?"

"Some." I didn't say more since there were a few patrons on the other side of the cafe, enjoying coffee and their books.

"What'll you have?" Connor asked.

"A double-boosted latte and whatever you have with cheese."

"Cheese quiche and a latte coming right up."

"Thank you. You're a hero." I tugged off my jacket and collapsed into my favorite seat, leaning my head back against the chair. Though I didn't normally experience jetlag from my cross-world jaunts, this time I was ready for bed. And it was only three in the afternoon. There would not be time for that, however.

Sighing, I pressed my fingertips to the comms charm at my neck. "Cass, you there?"

"Yeah, where are you? We should talk."

"P & P."

"Cool. We'll be there soon."

I cut the connection just as the door swung open and cool air rushed in. Ares, Del, and Roarke entered, making a beeline for me. They tugged off their jackets and sat.

Connor came over, carrying a tray with my quiche and latte. He smiled at the newcomers. "Hey, guys, what'll it be?"

I ate quickly while they ordered, ravenous. Connor wrote down their requests and left.

"Cass and Aidan will be here soon. We can do a recap," I said.

The door opened at that moment, and Cass and Aidan walked in, hair disheveled and foreheads slightly bruised.

"What happened to you guys?" I asked.

Cass flopped into a seat, shoving her red hair back from her battered face. "Well, we slammed into some kind of magical wall while looking for Alton."

I frowned. "That's not good."

"Nope." Cass shook her head. "When I transported, I couldn't get there. Slammed right into a wall."

"That's strange. Do you have any idea why?" Ares asked.

"Protection charm of some sort, we think," Aidan said. "Though I've never seen the likes of it."

"Which means it's freaking rare." I frowned. If it was security related, Aidan would know.

"We'll figure it out," Cass said. "What about you. How did Norway go?"

Del chuckled. "About how you'd expect Norway to go. Everything was bigger than life, including the magic. And it was cold."

"It's been a long two days," I said. "But we did get to meet a Valkyrie."

Cass grinned. "Very badass. They're super rare."

"Yeah. She was awesome. Though the news she shared was not." My stomach turned, thinking of my village. I explained everything that Hildr had told us, down to the last detail.

"Oh, shit, I'm sorry about your village," Cass said.

"Don't be. We'll save them," I said. "We just have to find that power source and the conduit. And Alton. We can't forget about him."

"This is the worst timing," Del said. "We need all our forces on Nix's problem, but we can't ditch a friend."

"Definitely not," I said. "The FireSouls have always come to our aid."

"Which means we now need to divvy up our resources and come up with a plan," Ares said.

I leaned back in my chair, sipping my latte. What to do first? I looked at Cass. "Why don't you try taking me and Del to the place where you think Alton is? Maybe we'll be able to recognize something."

"Sure. Though I suggest a hockey mask."

I grinned, then stood. "Let's do it now."

Cass nodded and joined me. Del stood as well. I glanced at everyone else. "We'll be right back."

I reached for Cass's hand. Del wrapped her arm around Cass's waist so that Cass could cover her face with her arm. Del and I mirrored the movement, and Cass dragged us into the ether.

I slammed into something hard and fell on my butt. As I got my wits about me, something familiar tugged. I opened my eyes to see the familiar dark grey dome that covered Elesius. "Crap."

I turned, looking for Cass and Del. They were climbing to their feet.

Cass's eyes were wide. "We didn't see this before. We just

slammed into a barrier and were spat back out into Magic's Bend." She approached the barrier, lifting a hand.

"Don't!" I grabbed her shoulder. "That's the barrier that's freezing Elesius."

Cass turned to me. "This is your home?"

"Yeah."

"No wonder we couldn't make it before. We couldn't cross over the barrier into Elesius when we tried to find you last week."

Del nodded, understanding glinting in her eyes. "But we can at least come here now because we're with Nix. And we're on the outskirts."

I searched the woods, the familiar huge trees towering around me. These weren't dead like the ones in Elesius, though they didn't look as healthy as normal trees. We were in the forest, away from town. The dome was huge, covering not just the city but the surrounding terrain as well.

"So Alton is somewhere in this forest," I said.

"But why?" Cass asked.

"I have no idea." I shivered, not liking that this was all part of the same terrible plot. "But it's no coincidence."

"Nope." Cass frowned. "We need to get started on our search, but this area is huge. I don't feel him nearby."

"Neither do I. My dragon sense feels weird. Scrambled, almost."

"Do you think it's the magic in the dome?" Del asked.

"Could be. Something is way wrong with this forest. Can you guys feel it?" I asked.

"Yeah, feels dark." Del spun around, eyes wide. "Did you hear that?"

The trees rustled. Hair stood up on my arms. A shadow darted amongst the trees twenty meters away, coming closer. To my left, thudding footsteps sounded. They were fast, and it was more of a gallop than that of a person walking. My eyes darted frantically, searching for both threats. I caught sight of the massive four-legged beast to the right. It had huge horns and looked a bit like a wild pig. A Boarhunde. To the left, a shadowy dark figure raced through the trees, white fangs gleaming in the dark. I'd never seen his kind before. And I didn't want to see any more. Both charged toward us, coming from different directions.

I raced toward Cass. "Let's get out of here."

"Hell, yeah." She grabbed Del and me, gripping tightly.

The ether sucked us in, throwing us across space. We stepped out in Magic's Bend, right in front of P & P. I sagged.

Del looked at us, eyes wide. "What the hell were those things?"

"Monsters of some kind." I drew in a shuddery breath.

"Did you know they lived near your town?" Cass asked.

"I had no idea."

We hurried into P & P. Ares, Aidan, and Roarke all stood, concern creasing their brows.

"You look like you saw a ghost," Ares said.

"More like monsters." I described what I'd seen, the enormous creature that had looked like a giant boar with massive horns and the shadowy creature that had looked like a nightmare version of a vampire.

"Hmmm." Ares rubbed his jaw and sat.

We all followed suit. My breathing was finally starting to calm.

"So this means that Alton is somewhere on the outskirts of your village. Which is no coincidence," Ares said.

"Exactly. Drakon has something to do with his abduction," I said.

"And we have to search the perimeter, but there are monsters," Cass said.

"A security measure, perhaps," Aidan said. "To make it difficult to find and interfere with what Drakon has planned."

"Makes sense." I leaned back in my chair, thinking. "We can't search on foot. We'll be too slow. We need off-roading vehicles."

"None of yours will work, then," Cass said.

"No." Mine were road-only, sports cars built for speed and not crazy terrain. "But I do know a couple people who could help."

Ares's gaze met mine. "Bree and Ana, from Death Valley?"

"Exactly. Their vehicles are built for rough terrain, and they've got the skills."

"Do you have the magic to transport the vehicles there, though?" Ares asked.

I nodded. I hadn't yet shown him my trove, or the cars that were on the roof of the factory building, but I knew a guy who could transport large objects like that. "We have to go find them."

"Do you think they'd do it?" Cass asked.

I thought about the tough, danger-loving girls who reminded me so much of Cass, Del, and me. "For the right price, yeah."

# CHAPTER ELEVEN

Ares and I transported directly to Death Valley Junction. The sun blazed overhead, warm and bright in the late afternoon. We arrived in the same place we had before, but at least we knew where we were going. As it had been before, it was quiet on the main road, people staying out of the sun during the heat of the day.

"Here's hoping they aren't out in the valley," Ares said as we set off down the street.

"Seriously." We passed by the old wooden saloons and the buggies parked in the alleys. It was the presence of the crazy cars that modernized the place a bit. Otherwise, I'd expect John Wayne to come strolling out the swinging doors of Death's Door Saloon.

As we neared the end of the main street, approaching the road where Bree and Ana lived, I noticed a figure standing close to the corner of a building, using the cover to spy on Bree and Ana's house. I nudged Ares in the side and pointed.

He studied the man, frowning, then murmured, "Suspicious."

"My thoughts exactly." That guy had stalker written all over him—but skilled, dangerous stalker. He wasn't the fumbling sort who was obsessed with a pretty girl.

I walked closer to his side of the street, approaching him. I didn't know what I planned to do when I reached him, but I wanted to get a better look. Maybe get a feel for his magical signature and figure out what the hell he was.

He stiffened, seeming to sense my approach, then vanished without turning around.

"He didn't want me to see his face," I said.

"Yeah. And he was hiding his magical signature."

I nodded. A complete lack of magical signature was rare, unless this guy was a human or an extremely powerful supernatural. And he was definitely no human.

We continued past the turn and saw Ana and Bree's house. Fortunately, their buggy was out front. The curtains by the front window twitched. They were watching.

I waved.

The door swung open a moment later, and Bree propped herself against the doorjamb. Her dark hair gleamed in the light, and she wore the same style strappy leather top that was very *Mad Max* chic.

"Don't tell me you want another ride across the valley."

"No." I approached. "But we do need your help."

She jerked her head back toward the interior of the house. "Come on in."

We followed her into the small, dark space. It was totally run-down, with very sparse, ragged furniture and window cracks covered with duct tape. Given what these girls charged for a ride across the valley, they couldn't be this broke. Even their buggy couldn't eat up all the money they made.

No way I'd be asking about it, though, since I certainly didn't want anyone asking where I put all the money I made from my shop.

Bree led us toward the small Formica table in the kitchen, shouting out toward the back of the house, "Ana! Get out here!"

We sat, and I looked at Bree. "There was a man watching your house."

She twitched, eyes nervous. "Yeah?"

"Yeah. Don't know what he was, but he could transport."

She shifted, clearly nervous but trying to hide it. Too young. In a few years, she'd be better at it. Cass, Nix, and I had only really gotten our poker faces after years of practice.

"Do you have a stalker?" Ares asked.

"Not that I'd tell you about." Her face closed up.

"Who's poking in our business?" Ana's voice came from behind.

She entered the kitchen, wearing a similar outfit to Bree's. Her blonde hair was no longer in a mohawk, but rather swept to the side in an artful disarray.

"Hi, Ana." I waved. "Not poking, just trying to help."

"We don't need help."

I shrugged, knowing when to let a bone go. "How about a job, then?"

Her eyes sharpened and she sat. "What kind of job?"

"We need you and your buggy to take us through a forest that is protected by monsters."

"Why?" she asked.

"We're looking for something, and we can't do it on foot. You're the only people we know with machines fast and rugged enough to give us a shot."

"How far away is it?" Bree asked. "We've got a job in two days. Can't miss it."

"It's in France. But I've got a guy who can transport your buggy there and then get them back out."

Ana's brows rose. "Must be a strong guy."

"Yeah, he is. Your buggy will be safe. And I'll pay you seventy-five thousand dollars."

Ana's eyes popped, then she coughed, trying to hide her reaction. Ares looked at me, interest clearly in his eyes. Damn. He was probably wondering how I had that much money lying around when I lived in such a dump. No one realized how well we did with our shop since we ferreted away all our money into our troves. Though Ares knew I was a FireSoul, I hadn't shared that with him yet.

Maybe it was time. Just the idea made me shiver. It was so personal... almost like sex, in a way.

I shoved the thought away, looking from Bree to Ana. "What do you say?"

The two girls looked at each other, indecision clear on their faces. They obviously liked their familiar stomping grounds. And Death Valley Junction was a hideout, no question. You didn't live here unless you had no choice. Sure, these girls clearly liked the adventure. But so did Del, Nix, and I. But as soon as we'd gotten enough money and the protection of some powerful concealment charms, we'd moved straight to a nice town and a nice apartment.

Would my offer be enough to overcome their wariness?

"Eighty-five and you've got a deal," Bree said.

Ana nodded resolutely, jaw set. "Not a penny less."

I winced. Seventy-five was the last of my stash from our most recent big sale. I'd have to get the rest off of Nix and Del, but they wouldn't mind.

"It's fine," Ares said. "You'll have your money right away. And we'll leave tomorrow morning."

I glanced at him and smiled. His gaze flicked to me, and he nodded so slightly I almost didn't notice.

"Fine," Ana said. "We'll do it. The money should be in our account tonight, and we'll be ready to go in the morning."

Bree saluted. "Limo drivers at your service."

I cracked a smile and stood. "Thanks."

"Just pay us. We don't need thanks."

I nodded and turned to leave, Ares at my side. At the door, I turned back. "That guy who was watching you. If you need help, you can come to us."

The girls scowled, distrust clear on their faces.

"Just pay us," Bree said.

"And be on time," Ana added.

I nodded and we left, stepping out onto the bright street.

"They're like feral cats," Ares murmured.

"Hiding from something," I said. "Those girls aren't FireSouls, but what they really are, or what they're hiding from, I have no idea."

"You can't save someone who doesn't want to be saved." Ares stopped and reached for my hand, ready to transport.

"That doesn't stop me from wanting to."

He leaned forward and kissed my forehead. "One of the things I like about you."

～

Later that evening, after finalizing plans for the next day and transferring the money to Ana and Bree, I let Ares into my apartment. We'd grabbed dinner at P & P—more cheese quiche and pasties because we were tired and lazy—and Ares had asked if he could spend the night here rather than heading back to the Vampire Realm.

It'd taken me only half a second to decide. Though I was worn out, I wanted him with me.

Ares followed me into the kitchen, where I headed to the cupboard and took down two glasses. "Bourbon do for you?"

"Anytime."

I poured us two glasses and handed one over. He sipped, clearly liking my Four Roses.

"I'm going to shower, then I've got something to show you."

His brows raised. "Yeah?"

"Yeah." I turned and walked toward the bathroom, my heart thundering at the idea. I was going to show him my trove—and no, that wasn't a dirty joke. It felt scary, but right. Maybe it was seeing Bree and Ana and how scared they were. How untrusting.

I'd been like them for so long. But I wanted to be different now. Embrace life without running and hiding.

From now on, if I was going to run, it was going to be at something, not away.

I didn't take long in the shower, just doing the bare minimum to get clean. When I left the little room, Ares stood from the couch.

"If you don't mind, I'll shower, too."

"Sure." I headed toward the bedroom to get dressed, but turned at the entrance. "There's a door in my bedroom. I'll leave it open, so when you're done, come up."

Interest glinted in his eyes. "All right."

The water turned on, a dull roar that was easy to hear through the thin walls of the apartment. Immediately, I thought of Ares naked. I'd never seen him that way, but it wasn't hard to paint a picture. It was every hot guy I'd ever seen in underwear ads, though I had a feeling that even that wouldn't do Ares justice.

*Head out of the gutter.*

I focused on selecting some PJs, then left the light on in the bedroom and ascended the stairs to my trove. As soon as I entered, I heard the fluttering of wings.

"Jeff?"

He popped his head up from between some ferns, onyx eyes staring at me.

"How you doing, buddy?" I held out a hand, and he came forward to give me a sniff of greeting. "You have a good day?"

His head moved a bit, which I took to be a nod. "Thanks for the help in Norway."

He nodded again.

Footsteps sounded on the steps leading to my trove. I stiffened, heart suddenly going wild.

Why had I decided to do this?

The door creaked open behind me, and I turned. Ares stood there, hair wet from his shower and impossibly handsome. Jeff, who fluttered at my side, disappeared immediately, as if he sensed the tension in the room. As if he sensed what might happen here.

He was my wingman. With wings. Giving me space.

"Hey," I said.

Ares's gaze traveled over the greenhouse, stopping briefly on the cars, then continued on. Awe shined in his eyes. "What is this place?

"My trove." I petted the leaf of a fern, drawing comfort from the plant. "Some FireSouls have them. We fill them with what is valuable to us. Our treasure."

"This is amazing. How did you get the cars up here?"

"I have a friend. Kelly. She's the strongest transporter there is. She's the one I called to help us with the buggies tomorrow."

"Ah, smart." He touched the stalk of a palm tree. "You've always liked plants."

"I have, though I didn't know why for a long time."

Ares came to join me, standing close and studying the shining green ferns on the table near my waist. "It's amazing."

"Thank you. I've worked a long time on it. For most of my life, I wasn't able to have a garden. We were running too much. Hiding."

"They were hard years."

I nodded, my heart suddenly aching at the tenderness in his expression. I swallowed hard.

"Thank you for showing me," he said.

"Yeah." The words stuck in my throat. This was too much attention, all focused on me and my secrets and my past. So I turned it on him. Cruelly, almost. But I was desperate. I needed the attention elsewhere. "Aethelred the Seer said you would lose what you love most. What is that?"

His face shuttered.

"I'm sorry." I touched his shoulder, suddenly—and rightfully— feeling like shit for putting him under scrutiny. "I was feeling... Um. I'm just not used to this. Feeling like this for someone and being the center of attention."

His gaze softened, and he reached up to cup my cheek. "You're going to have to get used to it. Because you *are* the center of my attention. You have been since the moment I met you."

I swallowed and nodded, touched.

Ares took my hand and tugged me away from the table. "Show me your amazing trove."

I smiled. "All right."

We walked amongst the rows, and I pointed out all of the plants, every one of them a favorite. The trees, the flowers, the ferns, the succulents.

"You've done incredible work here."

I squeezed his hand. "A labor of love."

Ares stopped at the Firebird, inspecting its sleek lines and bright red paint. He ran his fingertips over the side, toward the trunk, and I shivered. It was like he was touching me.

"This is beautiful." His gaze was hot, but it wasn't on the car.

I nodded, my mouth suddenly dry. My brain might not have known what to do, but my body did. I approached, standing in front of the trunk.

"Any reason you chose these cars?" he asked.

I shrugged, struggling for words. "I liked them. They each have their reason. But really, at the end of the day, I just liked them."

"I like you."

"Yeah?"

He crowded close. I held my ground. Which was a good thing, because the car at my back kept me from backing up anyway.

Ares propped both hands on the trunk, caging me in. My breath caught at his closeness, his heat.

"This is a sexy car." His big hands wrapped around my waist, and he lifted me, setting me on the trunk. "And you are one sexy woman."

He crushed his lips to mine. I gasped, then returned the kiss, reveling in his taste and touch. My heart thundered in my ears as he stepped closer, and I parted my legs to let him near.

He groaned, wrapping his arms around my waist and pulling me tight to him, his lips avid on mine. My breath grew short, and heat streaked through my veins. I stroked the hard muscles at his shoulders and arms.

"You feel amazing," I murmured against his lips.

"Not half as good as you do." He loosened his grip, running his hands down my back towards my hips. He gripped me there, tugging me toward him, and I gasped at the contact, sinking my hands into his hair and devouring his kiss.

His grip was tight on my hips, his hands firm, yet trembling with want.

I'd never been wanted so much that I made another person *shake*.

It made me feel powerful. And I liked it.

My head spun as he trailed his lips down my neck. His tongue burned me, but he was careful to keep his fangs away.

I ached for them, tilting my head to press my neck toward him.

He groaned. "What are you doing?"

"I want you to," I moaned.

"Want me to what?"

He was going to make me say it. I swallowed hard. "Bite me."

He shuddered against me, breath harsh. "Next time."

"Now."

He shook his head, then tilted my head up. His gaze was hot on mine, desperate. "I don't have the control now."

"I trust you." I pulled him toward me, pressing my body full against his.

His jaw clenched. "I don't trust myself."

"I want it."

He grinned, a wicked smile. "I can make you want something else."

I was about to ask, but then he dropped to his knees and I didn't have breath for any more words.

~

*All around me, the forest died. Slowly, quickly—it depended on the plant. But death was all around as the life leeched from my beautiful grove. The violets withered, and the leaves fell from the tress. Sunlight sparkled through the gaps in the canopy, a normally lovely sight turned dark by knowledge of what had caused it.*

*My heart raced and my skin chilled as I dunked my bucket into the stream, scooping up water. I lugged the bucket toward the base of a nearby oak, my arms burning from the strain. I poured the water onto the dirt.*

*"Go!" my mind cried. "Feed my beloved trees."*

*I didn't wait for the water to absorb. Instead, I spun back toward the stream and raced for it, refilling my bucket. The water glittered clear and bright, a horrible reminder that it was not drought that killed my forest. And that my actions were probably pointless. The ground was not parched, yet my forest had died.*

*And I didn't know how to save it. This wasn't a place that required fertilization or pruning. It was wild, natural. Able to live on its own.*

*Until now.*

*Now, it was dying, and there was nothing I could do to stop it.*

*I sobbed as I raced toward another tree, dumping my burden onto the ground and continuing on my way, back toward the stream. Sweat and tears poured down my face, burning my eyes. My muscles screamed.*

*My forest died.*

*In the distance, the familiar blue glow of the forest spirit watched me. She'd appeared when the trees began dying, haunting this place like a specter from a Gothic novel.*

*I turned toward her to get a better look, but she disappeared. The memory of her expression, the sadness etched into the lines at the sides of her mouth and her furrowed brow, burned into my mind's eye.*

# CHAPTER TWELVE

I woke with a gasp, tears streaming down my cheeks.

Next to me, Ares bolted upright, turning. "Nix!"

He pulled me close, and I buried my face against his shoulder, tears blinding me. Comfort surged through me, warm and bright.

"What is it?" Ares stroked my hair.

"Just a nightmare." I drew in a shuddery breath. Why the hell did I have to have one after the best night of my life?

"Do you have them often?"

I shook my head. "Not anymore. But this one... It was new."

"What was it?"

"I was killing the forest at Elesius. Whatever I did to try to save it...didn't work. Because *I* was the one killing it."

"You aren't."

"But I am, Ares. Even though fate decreed it and I didn't choose it, I still am." Which was one reason I wasn't super keen on fate right now. My life being on the line sucked, but killing my whole town? That *really* sucked. "The only way for me to save it is to return there to live for good. And I don't want to do that. I'd have to leave Cass and Del and Ancient Magic."

"They're your family now." He rubbed my arm.

I burrowed into his shoulder. "Yeah. We've been together since we were only fourteen. Every hard time and good time was with them. I don't want to leave them."

"There may be another way."

"Not according to my family in Elesius."

He squeezed me to him. "I'll help you. We'll find a way."

It was a pretty fantasy, but I grabbed onto it anyway. Freaking out about my future wouldn't help my present. And my present needed all the help it could get.

I kissed him on the cheek, then climbed out of bed. "Thank you."

"Anytime." Ares looked handsome as sin in the rumpled sheets.

Last night had been amazing. Rounding all the bases amazing, even without the biting that I'd demanded.

I whirled away to hide my blush. "We'd better get dressed. We have to meet Kelly soon."

Ares climbed out of bed. "All right. I'll meet you in front of P & P in twenty minutes. I need to go back to my place to change."

I nodded, then turned around. He stood just a couple of feet away. I leaned toward him, standing up on my toes to press a kiss to his lips.

I pulled away and smiled up at him. "Thank you for last night. It was pretty much the best one ever."

He pressed another kiss to my lips, then to my cheeks, and finally my forehead. "I'm fairly certain I should be thanking you."

"Hmm, I think I owe you more thanks. You should start a tab."

"A tab?"

"I don't mind paying it off."

A devastatingly sexy smile tugged at his lips. My body responded, heating up. I shook my head and stepped back. "You, sir, are dangerous. I need to go get dressed before I do something that I definitely don't have time for."

"We'll make time later."

"I like the sound of that."

~

Thirty minutes later, I waited outside of P & P with a cup of coffee warming my hands. I'd scarfed down a cheese scone while Connor had brewed my latte. He'd asked if I needed backup on this expedition, and while I probably did, there just wasn't room in Bree and Ana's buggy.

"Nix!" Cass's voice sounded from down the street.

I turned. She and Del were hurrying toward me, their usual battle gear on. Leather jackets for both of them—brown for Cass and black for Del—while Cass wore jeans and Del wore leather pants.

I eyed their outfits. "Guys. You can't come. There's no room for you in the buggy."

They both scowled. Though none of us were blood related, they sure looked like sisters in that moment.

"One of us can fit," Cass said. "You said it was a Hummer. Those things are freaking land yachts."

I hesitated. She was right. "One person."

"Dibs." Cass grinned at Del.

"Hey!"

"You went last time," Cass said.

Del sighed. "Fine. But if you need backup, you can transport and come get me. Deal?"

"Deal." Cass shook on it.

"Thanks for being willing to throw yourselves into danger, guys." I smiled at them, my heart warmed.

"Always." They spoke simultaneously.

Sometimes it was clear that we spent a hell of a lot of time in each other's company. Maybe too long. It was probably a good thing we all had boyfriends now. We'd been on our way to being a trio of cat ladies. Which wouldn't bother me too much, as I

141

liked cats. But I liked Ares better. And I was certain they liked Aidan and Roarke better as well.

Magic crackled on the air. I turned to face it, not surprised when Kelly popped out of thin air. I hadn't seen her since she'd transported the Firebird, my most recent car, into my trove, but her hair was blue this time. Pink streaks gleamed throughout. She wore a cool leather jacket studded with silver spikes. Very punk.

I grinned and held out my hand to shake. "Thanks for coming, Kelly."

She shot me a wide grin, her brilliant white teeth flashing. "Anything for you, darlin'."

Ares appeared on the sidewalk a half second later, dressed in clean jeans, dark shirt, and a beat-up brown leather jacket. It looked damned good on him.

"Just in time." I made the introductions with Kelly and explained that Cass was coming along.

"And you're picking me up if you need backup," Del said.

I saluted. "Be ready."

She nodded.

I turned to Ares. "Ready to head out?"

"Yes." He looked at Kelly. "Do you know Death Valley Junction?"

"I do. Go there for poker every third Thursday. Nothing like playing cards in the real old west."

It didn't sound like a bad way to spend an evening, actually.

"Then let's get out of here," Ares said. "We'll meet on the main street."

He reached for my hand. The ether sucked us in, spitting us out on the main street in Death Valley Junction. A half second later, Cass appeared next to me. Then Kelly. It was convenient to have so many people who could transport.

As expected, the street was dead quiet this early in the morning. Death Valley Junction probably saw some late nights with all the saloons in town.

"This way." I led the way down the street toward Bree and Ana's house.

They were waiting out front when we arrived, seated on their stoop. Each wore a pair of aviation goggles on their heads and were already wearing their hiking harnesses. They stood, each looking like a teenage badass in their leather. Though in truth, it wasn't the clothes. It was the wary look in their eyes and the fighters' stances.

"Déjà vu," Cass muttered to me.

"Right? All they need is a third." I approached them. "Thanks for being ready."

"Gotta be pro." Bree stuck her hand out to Cass. "I'm Bree."

"Cass."

They shook and Bree moved over to Kelly, introducing herself. Ana did the same, starting with Cass.

"So you're going to transport the buggy?" Ana asked Kelly.

"That's the plan. Then I'll leave you to it and pick you up again when you call."

"All right." Bree gestured us toward the buggy. "Come on."

The thing looked just as I remembered it. A hulking beast of metal and rubber, the spikes that jutted off the sides gleaming in the early morning sun. The small platforms over the front and back of the car had been given an extra safety bar.

We all climbed in, Ana behind the wheel and Bree next to her. Ares took the back platform, while I sat in the back seat between Kelly and Cass.

Bree turned around and gestured to the back seat floorboard. "Harnesses down there if you want them."

"Thanks." I reached down and grabbed one, then handed it back to Ares. I grabbed the other and strapped it on, ready to take on the challenges that protected Drakon's miserable operation at Elesius.

Cass did the same, asking, "What are these for?"

"If you want to fight from the platforms, you wear a harness," Ana said. "That way, if you go overboard, you don't go far."

"Smart." Cass strapped hers on.

"We like to think so," Bree said.

Kelly rubbed her hands together and grinned gleefully. "Ready to go?"

"Ready," Ana and Bree said in unison.

Kelly's magic swelled on the air, feeling like a fierce wind against my face. She reached out and placed her hands on the back of the front seats, closing her eyes. I touched Kelly's shoulder, envisioning Elesius. Except this time, I pictured the forest right outside the smoky barrier.

Magic vibrated through the car, Kelly's power filling the thing with magical energy. A moment later, the ether sucked us in, spitting us out in the woods. We were right next to the smoky barrier, fortunately. Not near the city entrance where Ares and I had discovered the barrier, but in a more remote section. The whole dome was massive, covering parts of the mountains and valleys as well as the city. We might have to drive a long way around to find Alton and Drakon.

"Perfect," I said. "Thanks, Kelly."

She handed me a small golden pebble. "Press that with your thumb to call me when you're ready. It'll take about thirty seconds for me to find you and arrive, so you've got to stay in the same position during that time. *Don't move.*"

"All right." I nodded and she disappeared.

Ana and Bree studied the forest around us. I tried to see it through their eyes, unencumbered by my love and sorrow for this place. Even with a neutral mindset, it was still amazing. The trees were massive—not quite as big as redwoods, but still huge. There was enough room between them that the buggy would be able to navigate the forest, but it'd take some expert driving. Fortunately, we had that in spades.

But the forest was silent. No birds or insects. Not even the rustle of winter wind through the leaves.

"Don't like it here," Bree murmured.

"Nope." Ana turned around to study the forest behind us. "Can't see what's coming. Not like in the desert."

"Does this thing have a stealth feature?" I asked.

Ana arched a brow. "Does it look like we're running some kind of amateur operation here?"

Bree chuckled, then hit a black button on the dash. When Ana cranked on the car, it vibrated with the rumble of the engine, but there was no sound. It was quiet as a Tesla.

"Lead the way, boss," Ana said.

"Straight ahead. Follow the dome around. We're a ways off, but this was as close as I could get us to the target."

"How do you find it?" Ana asked.

"Seeker sense," I lied. Though something told me I could trust these girls—I had an eye for honor—it wasn't worth the risk. "But the specific location is being protected."

"By more than just a spell," Cass said. "Keep an eye out for monsters. We saw two last time. Giant Boarhunde and some kind of creepy, shadowy vampire thing." She looked back at Ares. "No offense to your vampire half."

He smiled, unconcerned. "None taken."

Ana pressed on the gas, navigating around the massive trees with the hazy dome on our left. Bree climbed up on the front platform, hooking her harness to the safety bar. Ares stayed on the rear platform, while Cass and I stood on the back seat, our eyes alert on the forest. I scanned the trees, searching for any sign of life or threat. There wasn't so much as a squirrel or a robin sitting in the partially barren trees.

The thundering of hooves came almost as a relief. I'd been waiting, tensed for the first obstacle, and at least it sounded familiar.

"Boarhunde," Cass said. "Coming from right side."

I perked my ears. She was right. I could just make out the direction from the sound. Bree knelt on the front platform, her magic flaring as she readied herself. I conjured my bow, my heart pounding. Boarhundes were fast and mean.

The thing crashed through the trees forty meters away, as big as a city bus and almost as fast. Ana turned the buggy left, swerving behind trees, but the foggy gray dome surrounding my city blocked our escape.

I drew back on my bowstring, but hesitated. I hated to kill him. Perhaps wounding....

I fired, aiming for the Boarhunde's leg. A magical beast like him would heal more quickly, but at least it would keep him from attacking us. The arrow whistled through the air, straight and true. Then bounced off the beast's leg.

"Magically enhanced hide," Cass said.

The Boarhunde cantered alongside us, twenty meters off now, veering close enough to strike with his great horns. Fire blazed in his eyes, a black flame of determined rage. His horns were big enough that he could flip the buggy with them, then trample us with his great hooves.

My heart thundered. That'd be a terrible way to go.

Bree eyed the Boarhunde like a hawk. As soon as she had a clear shot, she threw out her hands. The sonic boom exploded out from her, striking the nearest tree instead of the Boarhunde. The tree half uprooted itself, slowing the Boarhunde but not striking it.

"Damn!" She scowled fiercely, then tried again. This shot nailed the Boarhunde in the back legs, bowling him over. He skidded on the ground, temporarily down. Long enough for us to get away, I hoped.

Bree scowled, clearly pissed at the miss.

Strange. I'd thought her more controlled with her magic.

"Shake it off," Ana said.

"Yeah." Bree scanned the forest like a hunter, looking for her next prey. It came in the form of two Boarhundes, each charging us with a ferocity that made the ground tremble with their steps.

Bree threw her sonic boom toward them, striking the first beast and sending it careening back against a tree.

"I gotta recharge!" Bree shouted.

The second Boarhunde was nearly on us, only fifteen meters away and galloping closer, its breath bellowing, somehow stinking up the air all the way over here.

Hoping to buy Bree some time, I fired my bow, sending arrow after arrow at the beast, faster than I'd ever done before. Each one bounded off the Boarhunde's hide. Cass's hands lit up with flame as she was about to throw a fireball, but Bree beat her to it, hurling a sonic boom at the beast. This one hit dead on, sending the monster skidding across the ground.

"Nice!" Ana called as she swerved around an upcoming tree.

She was right—Bree had done well. But clearly she was having a harder time away from her usual stomping grounds at Death Valley.

"Reminds me of me," Cass whispered.

"Yeah." Cass had once been totally unreliable with her magic —as likely to cause catastrophe as she was to save the day. For years, she'd hidden her gifts, not using them for fear of drawing attention to herself. FireSouls *never* wanted to draw attention. I'd suspected that there was a reason that Bree and Ana lived in Death Valley. This might've been it.

Fortunately, Ana could still drive like a pro, and Bree was no wimp. She'd charge the danger alongside her friend, reliable magic or no.

"Trees are getting closer together." Ana's voice was slightly worried. She cut through the biggest gaps, dodging and swerving.

"You've got this," Bree said.

I kept my gaze trained on the forest around us. It wasn't long before the vaguely familiar dark shadows appeared in the distance, zipping through the trees.

I pointed. "Shadow monsters!"

They flew through the trees, each seven feet tall and looking like grim reapers.

"Not Shadow monsters," Ares said. "Nosferatu. They'll tear your throat out and devour your soul."

Oh, hell no. I shivered. They were the terrifying stuff of nightmares. I'd only ever heard of such awful beasts, never seen one in real life before.

There were dozens of them, all converging upon us as a mass. They were fast—as fast as the buggy. But they didn't come straight for us. Instead, they darted through the trees in a strange pattern. What the hell were they doing?

Ana careened the car away from them, directing us down a dip in the terrain and dodging trees as she tried to gain some distance. The car whizzed past trunks so close that the spikes on the side gouged the bark.

Ares unclipped his harness and leapt off the back of the buggy, charging the shadow monsters in the distance. They were about thirty meters away now, still darting through the trees in their same pattern.

Cass took Ares's place on the back platform, clipping off her harness and charging up her firepower. I drew back on my bow, aiming for the nearest Shadow monster. I fired at one who was about twenty meters away, but my arrow sailed right through him.

"Damn it!" That was two creatures impervious to my arrows.

Cass hurled a massive fireball at the same monster I'd tried for. It sailed right through.

"What the hell!" She tried again, hurling a larger bomb.

Nothing.

In the distance, Ares darted through the trees, as fast as the Nosferatu that he fought. His shadow sword whirled in his hand, slicing off heads and gutting the beasts around him.

"Looks like his blade works," Cass said.

The Nosferatu had grouped behind us, driving us away from the shadowy dome instead of towards it. *Why?* They could trap us if they corralled us against the dome.

*Trap us.* Realization hit me.

"Ana! They're corralling us!" Like mammoth hunters had corralled the mammoth so that they could kill it in the location of their choosing.

"Where?" Ana scanned the surrounding terrain, searching for the oncoming threat. She had to drive slower and slower as the trees closed in. Soon, we weren't going more than twenty miles an hour. My heart thundered as the monsters gained on us.

Ares raced behind us, cutting through the monsters one by one, but they were still driving us away from the shadowy dome. I felt so damned helpless, my arrows worthless against their incorporeal forms.

Suddenly, the ground gave out from beneath us, a huge pit swallowing us up.

I screamed as we fell, but we thudded to the ground a moment later, the front of the buggy crashing into the side of the dirt wall. I slammed forward, the front seat gouging my side. Cass flew into the back seat, and Bree flew forward, her harness keeping her from going too far.

I scrambled upright, heart thundering. We were in a pit at least fifteen feet deep. I looked up, catching sight of the black-cloaked figures staring down at us. When they began to drop into the pit—*their trap*—my skin chilled. Though the light was dim here, it glinted off their long white fangs.

They converged on us. Visions of them tearing us apart flashed briefly in my mind.

Bree threw a sonic boom at the nearest Nosferatu. It flew right through him, blasting away the dirt wall behind.

*We couldn't fight them.*

Maybe my enchanted sword could, but I wasn't fast enough to take out all them before they got to my friends. I shoved aside the terror that roared free and called upon my magic, seeking the roots of the trees that threaded through the dirt around us. Their life force pulsed, drawing me toward them. I envisioned them bursting forth from the dirt.

They did as I commanded, massive roots surging out of the ground and lifting up the buggy. They twined around the mass of metal, lifting us out of the pit as the Nosferatu surged below. I could *feel* their thwarted rage.

"Whoo!" Ana howled as we were raised high into the air, out of the grip of the Nosferatu.

With our luck, they'd climb after us soon enough, but the reprieve was welcome.

On the surface, Ares sliced his blade across the neck of the last standing Nosferatu, then he leapt into the pit to finish off the rest. Though I wanted to join him and try out my new blade, I doubted my ability to be able to keep the vehicle in the air if I was distracted.

I leaned over the side of the buggy, peering down into the pit thirty feet below. The roots had taken my request seriously, hoisting us a good fifteen feet above the normal ground level.

"This is some badass power you have," Bree said.

I wanted to answer, but instead focused my magic on the roots as I watched Ares cut through the Nosferatu in the pit. As expected, he had no trouble. Now that they were all contained, it was quicker work. He slayed them all, twelve in total, in less than two minutes.

"Not bad," Cass said.

"No kidding." I directed the roots to lower the car to the ground. They set us down at the edge of the pit.

Ana scrambled out over the hood and inspected the damage to the buggy. Fortunately, a massive black metal grate covered the front.

"Minimal." Ana climbed back into her seat. "The grate protected the front."

Ares climbed out of the pit and leapt onto the back of the buggy.

"Nice work," Bree said.

Ares nodded, taking up a post next to me. Ana put her foot on the gas, directing the buggy back toward the foggy black dome surrounding our city.

"Why'd your sword work when my arrows didn't?" I asked.

"It was crafted specifically to defeat Nosferatu." He scanned the forest, searching for threats. "We had a plague of them five years ago in the Vampire Realm. This blade is the only thing that could defeat them."

"And it was wielded by you, I imagine?" I asked.

"Yes. But I had help. Doyen and Magisteria each have their own blade, and they're fierce in battle when they need to be. "

Yeah, I totally bought that. They might lounge around on their thrones if given the choice, but they were like coiled adders, ready to strike.

Ana steered the buggy around the dome.

"Are these monsters native to this area?" Ana asked.

"I don't know." I still couldn't remember everything about my homeland.

"I think not," Ares said. "Nosferatu are nearly extinct, and they generally don't live on Earth. They were brought here by an outside source."

"Drakon," I said. "They're his guards."

Ares nodded. "Most likely."

"Which means more are coming." I shivered. "Maybe not Nosferatu, but something."

"No doubt." Cass scanned the forest around us, searching for the threat.

We covered another few miles of ground, absorbing the eerie silence around us. Magic sparked in the air, a new signature that I hadn't felt before.

"I think we're getting close," I said.

"I feel that, too," Cass said.

The trees rustled, the first breeze we'd felt. The hair on my arms stood up. I shivered. The air was thick with tension. Thunder rolled on the horizon. I looked up. The sky was clear.

"Too blue," I murmured. There wasn't a cloud in the sky to make that thunder.

In the distance, between the trees, the air shimmered.

"Incoming." I didn't know what it was, but something was coming for us. And it wouldn't be good. The shimmering air coalesced to form a massive figure. A giant.

"Oh, shit!" Cass cried.

The beast was fifty feet tall if he was an inch, covered in heavy iron armor that concealed his form. Huge horns jutted from either side of his head. A massive club hung from his big hand. This guy's picture would be next to blunt force trauma in the dictionary. It was his footsteps that sounded like thunder. Though he was still sixty meters away, they shook the buggy.

"What is it?" Bree cried.

"A demon giant." Ares's voice was slightly tinged with dread.

I'd never heard that before. I climbed up onto the front platform next to Bree, trying for an unblocked shot.

"He's not close enough for my sonic boom," she said.

I knelt, taking aim, then released the string. The arrow flew straight for the beast's eyes, the only gap in his armor that I could see. It was only feet from him when he shifted his head. The arrow bounced off his helmet.

Ares leapt off the back of the buggy, racing toward the giant. His vampire speed far outstripped the buggy, which had to weave through the trees.

Ares neared the giant, who swung his club in return. The vampire leapt over the massive weapons, darting toward the giant's legs. He struck with his sword, but the blade clanged off the metal.

"Enchanted armor," Ana said.

*Shit.*

We couldn't just stand here.

The giant swung for Ares again, bending over far enough that I could see a small opening at the top of his helmet. It'd been damaged and not repaired. His Achilles heel.

I pointed. "Cass! Look!"

"I see it." As if she'd read my mind, her magic shimmered on the air, a signature so strong that Bree and Ana gasped. Cass might have once been terrible with her magic, but now she was the strongest Magica in the world.

"Drive around the giant!" I called to Ana as I turned to watch Cass jump out of the jeep and roll into a standing position. "Avoid the giant."

The air around Cass shimmered as she transformed into a griffon. Thank fates she'd stored up some magic from Aidan. As a Mirror Mage, she could mimic magical gifts when she was near a person, or she could store it up for a one-time use later on.

This was our one time, and we'd have to make it good.

Cass, in her griffon form, galloped alongside the buggy.

"Bad ass." Bree moved out of the way, giving me space to jump off the platform.

I landed on Cass's back with a thud. I'd swear I heard an *oof,* but Cass recovered from my ungraceful landing and took off into the air, flying high through the trees.

Ares raced around the giant, aiming for his legs. He caught sight of us above and grinned, then redoubled his efforts, distracting the giant.

Cass flew over the giant's head, hovering out of reach of his long arms and club. I leaned over her, taking aim with my bow. The gouged-out hole in his helmet was just big enough for my arrow, but it'd have to be the most perfect shot I'd ever accomplished.

When the giant's club hit Ares in the side, sending him flying through the trees, rage welled in me, sharpening my focus to laser precision. When the giant straightened from his blow, he gave me the perfect in. I released my arrow, which *finally* hit its mark, slicing through the hole and thudding into his skull.

The giant stopped dead in his tracks, swaying. Then he toppled over, shaking the forest floor with the weight of his fall.

"Get me to Ares!" I cried, but Cass was already wheeling in the air and flying toward him. She dodged the trees by inches, taking the shortest route.

Ana had diverted the buggy toward Ares. It pulled to a stop at his side as Cass landed on the ground near him. I scrambled off her back.

Ares was sitting up, wincing. I fell to my knees at his side. Though I couldn't see the damage since it was under his clothes, he was really favoring his right side.

"Are you all right?" I demanded.

"That was dumb, losing sight of the giant like that." He grimaced. "But I'm fine."

"Well, no one can say you aren't brave." I reached for his hand to help him up. Though he let me, he was clearly in better shape than I'd thought, surging to his feet.

"Just a few busted ribs," he said. "I've had worse."

"The vampire healing has to help, too." Bree's voice was wistful. "What a gift that is."

"Won't argue there." Ares climbed into the buggy. I followed. Cass shifted back to human and joined us.

"Ready?" Ana yelled.

"Yeah." I looked at Ares, who was already back up on the platform, broken ribs either forgotten or ignored.

Ana took off, sticking close to the barrier around my city. More magic sparked on the air, prickling against my skin. The buggy climbed up the side of a mountain, the terrain forcing us farther away from the dome surrounding Elesius.

"We've got to be close," Cass said.

"Yeah. No question." Not only was my dragon sense tugging

hard, but the air was prickling with protective magic. We were close enough that Drakon was really ramping up his protection charms.

"Looks like a valley up ahead," Ana said.

I stood on the back seat to get a better view. The buggy climbed slowly down the hill into a valley. The other side rose up into a mountain. The dome was to our left. At the top, blue magic shined, a bright glow that was unmistakable.

"Whoa." Cass leaned forward. "What the hell is that?"

I had no freaking idea. We were in a part of the woods that had an excellent view of our surroundings. I could even see the top of the smoky black dome from here. But it was the mountaintop across from us that had my attention. The magic glinted bright and blue, almost like a miniature dome formed of veins of blue light. It was roughly the size of a house, though scale was hard at this distance. At the top, it formed an arc of blue magic that traveled through the air, terminating at the top of the smoky black dome that froze Elesius. I squinted. It didn't actually terminate at the top. Rather, it sliced down into the city.

How was I supposed to use my enchanted sword through this?

"That's gotta be Drakon's device," I said.

"Slow the buggy," Ares said.

Ana complied. I conjured a pair of binoculars and trained them on the glimmering blue dome. It was formed of arcs of blue light, almost like static lightning. Within, there was an orb-like shape that glittered black, and a man.

I gasped. "Alton!"

# CHAPTER THIRTEEN

"Where?" Cass demanded.

"In the dome." I squinted, trying to determine if he was okay. He still wore his burnished red armor, though there was a deep gash on his cheek. The blood was now dried and dark against his face. "He's standing too still. Something is wrong with him."

"Gimme." Cass gestured for the binoculars. I handed them over, and she peered through. "Yeah, he's totally frozen. And that orb is weird. It's almost like a giant gemstone."

"We have to save him."

"There's no way to approach stealthily," Ana said. "It's all open terrain, especially in the valley."

I studied our surroundings. She was right. We were nearly into the valley, where the trees were thinner. A river cut through, leaving a big open patch that had no cover. The tree line on the other side was thick, a natural barrier that would be hard to get through in the buggy.

A ghostly figure appeared near the dome, slender and small. A woman?

Suddenly, figures broke from the trees. At least a few dozen of them, all mounted on horseback, charging toward us.

"Incoming!" Bree yelled.

Cass snapped the binoculars down to stare at the mounted attackers. "Demons! And demonic horses!"

And damn, were they fast. No sooner had Cass spoken than they'd leapt across the wide river and traveled twenty meters closer to us. I could now make out the horns on the heads of both the riders and the horses.

"There's at least forty," Ares yelled. "Retreat."

"Don't need to tell me twice." Ana turned the buggy in a tight circle and cut diagonally across the mountain behind us, speeding away from the smoky black dome and our oncoming attackers.

I climbed onto the back platform with Ares, budging him over to make room. The mounted demons charged toward us, unnaturally fast on their horses. They were gaining on us, able to ride faster than our vehicle could maneuver through the trees. Ana was fast, but there was no outracing the more maneuverable horses.

My heart thundered as I drew back the string on my bow. Out of the corner of my eye, I saw Ares clip my harness to the safety bar.

I fired, my arrow finding its mark in the eye of a demon. He flew back off his mount and crashed to the ground. I conjured another arrow and fired. Then again.

"Trade me!" Cass called to Ares.

He climbed down, and she scrambled up, conjuring her fire power and hurling a massive ball of flame at a demon that was breaking away from the pack. They were now only forty meters away.

They fired arrows and threw knives. I dodged one, but another sliced through the side of my thigh. Cass was struck in the shoulder with an arrow. She screamed, going to her knees.

"Faster!" I screamed.

"I'm trying!" Ana swerved through the trees, narrowly avoiding collision every time.

I fired my arrows as quickly as I could, my mind cold and precise even as my heart thundered like a drum and pain sliced through my leg.

In the buggy, it was hard to dodge the blades. An arrow plunged into Ares's arm, while Bree was sliced by a flying dagger that hit her shoulder.

But there were too many mounted demons, and they were too damned fast. The speed that the buggy could gain on open ground wasn't possible here in the thickest part of the forest. They gained with every second. There was only thirty meters of distance, then twenty. When they directed their mounts alongside the vehicle, my skin chilled.

"They're circling us!" Ana cried.

"We need to transport and leave the buggy!" Cass called.

"Hell no," Bree yelled. "You can bail, but we're not leaving our ride."

It was their livelihood. And they were stubborn.

I looked at Cass. As expected, she shook her head, refusing to leave them.

Bree shot her sonic boom at the nearest mounted demon. He flew off his horse and skidded in the dirt. But there were too many!

They raced ahead of the buggy, narrowing in to cut us off. We'd have to plow through them, but would we make it? More demons joined the first, their blades outstretched. They were only thirty meters ahead of us. Two of them unraveled a bright silver cable, stretching it across our path. It sparked with magic. They stretched it farther and farther, making it impossible to drive around.

"A Boom Thread." Ana took her foot off the gas, slowing the buggy to a crawl. "That'll blow us up in seconds."

"Oooh, shit." Cass hurled a fireball at the demons that were now twenty meters in front of us. The demon dodged, avoiding the blow by inches.

We were in so much trouble. Fear chilled my skin.

Familiar magic sparked on the air.

A huge green and white blur flew past us, hurtling straight for the demons.

Jeff!

And he was huge! As big as a horse.

Cass gasped. "Is that your dragon?"

"Yeah." I couldn't believe my eyes. He'd been growing, but this was extreme.

Jeff flew right for the demon holding one end of the Boom Thread. He blew out a huge bolt of fire, lighting up the demon like a torch and avoiding the horse. The fire must have triggered the magic in the Boom Thread, because it exploded in a spectacular show of lights and flame.

"Like the freaking Fourth of July," Cass said.

"Impressive," Ares murmured.

Jeff swooped amongst the demons, blasting them with his fire. They burst into flame, flailing. More than a dozen were barbecuing in front of us, a ghastly sight. The horses seemed to like it, however. They actually seemed to be eating it, snapping their heads back to lick at the flame. That was a relief. Even though they were hell horses, I hated to see them hurt.

The rest of the demons fled from Jeff, directing their mounts back toward the valley. More would come after us I was sure, but we had a brief reprieve.

"Go!" Bree yelled. "It's our opening."

Ana laid her foot on the gas, dodging between the trees and racing for the clearing. We needed to get far enough away from the other demons that we could call Kelly to transport us out of here.

Jeff flew past us, chasing the demons. He looked smaller than he had been. Almost the size of a large dog.

I spun around. "Jeff! Get back here!"

He whirled on the air, hurtling back toward me. He was definitely smaller. We sped past the burning bodies of the demons with Jeff flying alongside.

"He's smaller," Cass yelled.

"Yeah. No idea why." I gestured him over, and he flew right up beside us, then dived into the footwell. He landed with a thud in the corner, now the size of a house cat.

"You have a freaking dragon?" Bree cried.

"Yeah." I inspected him as the buggy bounced over the mountainside. He didn't look like he was shrinking any more, which was a relief.

"Call Kelly," Ares said. "We're far enough away."

"On it." I dug the charm out of my pocket and pressed it hard with my thumb.

Ana stopped the buggy. The air was dead quiet. Our ragged breathing was the only thing I could hear.

"Come on, come on," Ana muttered. She climbed onto the seat to scan the surroundings.

The air prickled with tension as we waited. The demons would regroup and come after us, especially now that Jeff was out of the picture. He'd actually fallen asleep in the corner of the seat, slumped against the cushions.

"I guess he used up his magic," Cass said.

"Yeah." I petted his head lightly. He snuffled.

"Incoming," Ares said.

I looked up. On the horizon, back the way we'd come, a group of mounted demons were charging toward us.

"Oh shit oh shit oh shit." Ana plopped back into her seat and revved the engine.

"No!" I reached out and grabbed her shoulder. "We have to wait for Kelly. This is our only shot. If we start running now, we won't be able to stop. She'll be here in seconds."

"Loooong seconds." She turned back around to watch the

demons, brow creased.

I swallowed hard and turned, watching them thunder toward us. *Come on, Kelly.*

It'd been almost forty-five seconds now. She'd said thirty. Where was she? My skin crawled, and my breath stopped. The demons were only forty meters off now.

"We're going to have to run for it," Bree said from her position on the front platform.

That second, Kelly appeared in the empty passenger seat.

"Go!" Ana cried. "Get us out of here."

Kelly's head whipped around, an unconscious reaction to the obvious panic in Ana's voice. Her eyes widened at the sight of the oncoming demons—which were only twenty meters off now. She threw her hands onto the seat of the car, and her magic welled.

Knives and blasts of fire began to land around us, thrown by the oncoming demons. Right before the ether sucked us in, I caught sight of the shadowy form of Drakon, flying high in the sky.

～

We appeared in Death Valley Junction a moment later. The hot sun beat down, and the silence was deafening. I slumped in the back seat next to Jeff, my adrenaline finally fading, leaving me shaky and weak. For a moment, all I could hear was the gasping breaths of my friends.

Ares leaned over me in the back seat. "Are you all right?"

I nodded, wincing at the deep pain in my leg. A quick inspection revealed a deep cut that wept blood. I glanced up at Ares. "You still have an arrow sticking out of your bicep."

He glanced down as if he'd forgotten, then snapped it in half and yanked it out. I winced, turning toward my friends. Bree was cradling her cut arm, and Cass had an arrow protruding from her shoulder.

"Let's get back to Magic's Bend." Cass's voice was strained. "I don't have the guts to yank it out myself. I'm going to go find Aidan."

She disappeared at that, using her transporting gift to go directly to Aidan, who would heal her.

"She's got the right idea." I struggled to sit straight, meeting Bree's gaze. "Are you all right? That wound looks ugly."

She nodded sharply. "I'll be fine."

"We have healers."

"So do we." She climbed out of the car, stumbling when she hit the ground. Ana leapt out and wrapped an arm around her waist. "And I'm going to go see her right about nowish."

"Thank you for the help!" I called after their quickly retreating figures.

The two waved, but didn't turn back.

"Girls of few words," Kelly said.

"That's them." I smiled shakily at her, pain and weakness making my stomach churn. "Thanks for the help."

She nodded. "That was a close call. I'm going to head out of here."

"Yep, us too." I waved goodbye to her then looked at Ares. "Now let's get out of here."

He nodded and wrapped an arm around my waist. I grabbed the sleeping Jeff, who was now the size of a house cat, and dragged him against my chest. He didn't wake, even when the ether sucked us in.

We arrived at the big green door leading to my apartment. Immediately, Del stuck her head out her window on the third story and shouted down. "You okay?"

"Yeah!" I winced when I tried to take a step.

Ares swept me up into his arms.

"Thanks." I sagged against him.

"That wound has sliced deep. Take it easy."

Del opened the green door, and Ares stepped inside, heading

up to my apartment. I was cradled in his arms, and Jeff was cradled in mine. We were like a weird Russian nesting doll.

Del pushed open the door so that we could walk through, asking, "Where's Cass? How'd it go?"

"It was okay." Pain made my breath short. "Cass went to find Aidan so he could heal her. We found Alton. Alert the FireSouls, will you?"

"Of course. Should they come here?"

Ares set me on the couch, and I slumped there. Jeff woke up and climbed off me, curling up on the far cushion.

Ares knelt by my side. "You've lost a lot of blood."

My head swam. I must not have noticed how bad it was during the fight—but then, adrenaline always made me fight through the pain.

Del leaned over me and gasped. "Yeah, that's a deep cut."

"Have the FireSouls meet us in a few hours for a recap," Ares said. "Nix will need to rest."

"I'm okay, I can—" I gasped at a strike of pain. "Yeah. Just a few hours. Be ready to fight."

I glanced at the clock on the side table. Three o'clock p.m. That would give me enough time.

"All right." Del hurried away. "I'll be back to check on you."

I waved, or at least tried to. My hand only moved a few inches off the couch cushion.

"I'm going to have to heal you," Ares said.

I nodded weakly. He raised his wrist to his lips, his white fangs extending. He bit, puncturing the skin, then withdrew his fangs. A strange hunger welled inside me as he raised his wrist to my lips.

"You'll heal better if you drink," he said, his voice raspy.

I nodded weakly, pressing my lips to the puncture wounds at his wrist. As soon as the warm blood hit my tongue, pleasure exploded through me, followed by light and strength. I moaned, drawing deep.

The blood was hot and sweet, delivering strength throughout my entire body. The pain dulled as the rest of me warmed.

Like last time, Ares's eyes burned hot and fierce. His lids dropped low as he watched me. Eventually, he raised his other hand to my jaw, pressing gently to release my bite.

"Careful, or you'll get drunk," he said.

I drew away, licking my lips. Exhaustion still pulled at me, but the pain was gone. I looked at my leg. The wound was quickly knitting itself back together, an eerie sight.

"Thank you." I gripped his hand.

"You need a few hours for the full effects."

I pulled him toward me, kissing him. His lips were firm and warm beneath mine. Despite the pleasure that made me moan, my vision grew even hazier.

He kissed me hard, a parting kiss, then picked me up in his arms. "Come on. We need to get you to bed. A few hours, and you'll be ready to fight anew."

I laid my head against his shoulder, the memory of the pleasure streaking through me. "That's not all I'm going to want to do anew."

He chuckled and laid me gently on the bed. I reached up and gripped his arm. "Stay."

He nodded. Whatever he said, I couldn't hear, as sleep was already taking me.

~

*I was in the forest again, on the outskirts of Elesius. I sprinted through the forest, darting between skeletal trees and leaping over exposed roots.*

*Where was she?*

*Frantic, I searched the area around me, looking for the only one who might be able to help me save the forest. All the water in the stream made no difference. Elesius had no shortage of water.*

*So something else was killing the forest. I just had to find her to help me save it. It felt like I sprinted for hours, my lungs burning and my muscles aching. But I couldn't stop. I couldn't. I couldn't.*

*Finally, in the distance, I caught sight of her. Her long white dress glowed in the dim light of the forest, and her pale hair cascaded down her back. I raced for her, drawing up short when I realized that she was nearly transparent.*

*"What happened to you?" I demanded.*

*She turned to me, beautiful as ever. The leaves that were her hair were no longer a pale green, but rather a faded white. And I could see through her body to the tree beyond. The sparkle in her eyes was the same, but that was all.*

*"Time." Her voice was wispier, weaker.*

*"I don't understand." I shook my head, horrified.*

*"You do not understand now, but you will." She started walking away from me, gesturing for me to follow. "But now is not the time for the past. It is time for the present. You must save Elesius, Phoenix."*

*"Save the forest? How? It is dying."*

*"Save it all." She led me toward the edge of the magical barrier that protected our town. But it was no longer the glimmering white that I was so used to. Instead, it was a hazy black smoke.*

*"What happened?" I reached for it.*

*"No! Don't! You do not have your sword."*

*"I have no sword."*

*"You will. When you return to save Elesius from Drakon, you will have the sword." She pointed to the hazy black mist of the barrier. "And you will sneak into the city here, through this weak spot."*

*"I have no idea what you're talking about." I stepped closer to the barrier, inspecting it.*

*She was right. The hazy black mist was weaker here. It was so transparent that I could make out the wide river on the other side of the barrier.*

*"You must hurry, Phoenix. We do not have much time. I created the weak spot in the barrier, but it will not last. You must save us."*

*I turned to ask her more questions, but she was gone. I was alone.*

# CHAPTER FOURTEEN

I gasped, bolting upright in bed. Ares was nowhere to be found. With a shaking hand, I turned on the bedside light. It shined golden. I blinked.

Ares popped his head into the bedroom. "Good, you're awake. The FireSouls will be at P & P in thirty minutes."

"What time is it?" I climbed out of bed, the wound in my leg no longer bothering me. A quick glance showed that it was gone. Ares must have pulled my dirty jeans off of me. He'd left the panties, of course.

"Nine. You've slept for a few hours."

"Perfect. That will give us a chance to attack before dawn. It's nine hours ahead there."

"I like how you think."

I smiled. "I'm going to shower. I'll meet you in the living room soon."

He nodded and left the bedroom. As I climbed into the shower, the dream raced through my mind. That woman had been familiar. She was the ghost I'd seen in the forest when I'd first arrived in Elesius last week.

At that time, I'd thought I'd never seen her before. But the truth was more complicated. If my dream was to be trusted, I'd known her before she'd faded away.

But who was she?

None of it made much sense, other than the fact that she'd definitely shown me a weak spot in the barrier trapping Elesius, and that my sword was supposed to be able to cut through it.

～

Thirty minutes later, Ares and I walked into P & P. It was warm and bright inside. Everyone was already gathered, chairs pulled up to form a big circle. All twelve FireSouls, my *deirfiúr* and their men, Connor and Claire, and even Aerdeca and Mordaca.

Connor had put carafes of coffee out on a table, along with trays of leftovers from the day. No time for custom orders now that we had a rescue operation to enact.

I'd just gotten a glimpse at everyone when the door opened behind me. I turned to see Bree and Ana enter.

I smiled. "What are you doing here?"

"We wanted to help you save your friend." Ana scowled. "It's not right, how he's trapped like that."

"Thank you. It could be deadly, though."

Bree shrugged. "Not a problem."

"Thank you." I turned back to the room. The twelve members of the League of FireSouls were all dressed in burnished red leather armor. Their gazes were hard. Ready.

Mordaca and Aerdeca were both dressed in black tactical wear, Aerdeca having forgone her usual white, no doubt knowing that we'd be attacking at night.

I took one of the closest seats, Ares at my side. Bree and Ana went to the food table and dug in.

"Thank you all for coming." I looked at Mordaca and Aerdeca. "Did Aethelred tell you we needed help?"

Aerdeca nodded. "He may have mentioned something." She caressed the sword sheathed at her hip. "And my blade is thirsty."

Mordaca just grinned, her lips the color of blood.

"You've found Alton," Corin said.

"We have. We're going to try to save him tonight. It's nine hours ahead in France, but we still have at least an hour of darkness to shield us."

"What's our plan?" Corin said. "Where is he? France?"

I explained to them what we'd seen. "So you can see that our odds are poor. Drakon has an army. It's dozens, probably more. Maybe hundreds."

"We didn't get a great look," Cass said.

"Too busy running for our lives," Bree added.

"Then we need stealth and cleverness," Fiona said. "Do you have a plan?"

"I do. But it could be a death sentence, depending upon how many warriors Drakon has. And how well I perform my part."

"We don't leave a FireSoul behind," Corin said. "We're in."

"All right, then." I nodded, then looked at Connor. "How much invisibility potion do we have?"

He studied the assembled crowd. "Enough for everyone, but only for about thirty minutes."

I nodded. "It'll have to be enough." I turned to the group. "Here's the plan..."

~

Since cars wouldn't be able to penetrate the thick tree line protecting Drakon's creepy blue lightning cage, we all transported one by one without vehicles. Several of the FireSouls were transporters, which helped.

I arrived in the valley below Drakon's mountaintop, along with Ares and Del. Within a minute, everyone else arrived. We'd already taken the invisibility potions, so speed was vital. We had to get into position before we became visible again.

All eyes turned to me. I nodded, giving everyone the thumbs-up. I caught Cass's eye, and she nodded back.

Then we turned and ran, racing toward the river. Del used her power over sound to muffle our footsteps. My breath heaved as we sprinted across the river, jumping from flat stone to flat stone.

On the other side, the group split. Ares accompanied me, my escort toward the smoky black barrier. Everyone else ran up the mountainside, determined to get as close to Alton as they could. They'd hide in the treetops and wait for my signal.

The dragons weren't here, but Jeff had done us a favor by killing so much of Drakon's army. There were more though—probably *a lot* more—and I prayed we'd make it out alive.

The moon was bright in the sky above, illuminating the form of the smoky black dragon that swooped above Elesius.

*Drakon.*

I swallowed hard, my skin chilling. I shook away the fear and ignored him, sprinting for the part of the barrier where the forest spirit had indicated I would find a weak spot. My dragon sense pulled me toward it.

When I reached it, I stopped, panting. I turned to Ares, then leaned up and kissed him hard. We didn't know if he'd be able to accompany me in because I was the only one wielding the sword that could cut through the mist, but I doubted it. He squeezed me once, then let go.

"Be safe," he whispered.

"You too."

I stepped up to the barrier. On the other side, I could see the faint flow of the forest spirit. She waited for me.

I drew the Valkyrie's sword from the sheath at my back and struck out for the barrier. My blade sliced through cleanly, leaving a gash. With a deep breath, I stepped through, turning back to face Ares.

As I'd expected, the black mist closed up again before he could enter. He reached for it, trying to force his hands through. He pushed and strained, but wasn't able to break through.

"Go." I could barely see his features, but I could *feel* his scowl. "I'll meet you at the battle."

He nodded, the motion hard to see, then turned and raced for the battle. With his superior speed, he should be able to make it into the trees before the invisibility potion wore off.

My blade seemed to cut through the spell, protecting me from the freezing charm, but I could see it all around me, a black haze on the air.

I turned to the forest, meeting the eyes of the forest spirit. She was very transparent, her white glimmering form the only point of light in the whole dark place.

"You don't have long," she said. "Come."

I followed her through the forest, toward the town. I couldn't see it yet, but my dragon sense told me that we were going in the right direction.

"Who are you?" I asked as we ran. Well, I ran. She kind of floated.

"The forest. You."

"That's not very clear," I whispered. I didn't think Drakon could hear me all the way down here underneath the smoky black dome, but maybe.

"You will understand." She raced ahead and I followed.

Running alongside her felt familiar. There was a connection between us.

"Are you the spirit of the forest?" I asked.

"In a sense." She slowed as we neared the base of the town, then pointed to the street that sloped upward along the valley ridge. The buildings crowded it on either side, turning it into a narrow alley. Lights gleamed on lampposts, illuminating the dark. "You will find the blue lightning at the top, in the court-yard. Your blade will do what it must."

"Have you seen my mother?" I had to know that she was all right.

"I have not." She made a shooing motion. "Now go. Your invisibility charm is fading, and you are running out of time."

"Thank you." I turned and ran, sprinting up the street.

As I passed by houses with their lights on, I saw the inhabitants, frozen inside. Everyone was stopped in mid-motion—eating, sitting, cleaning, walking. I shivered at the eeriness. There were even frozen people on the road.

I dodged them, hurrying toward the blue glow at the top of the street. The town was nearly silent save for the water that flowed through the fountains set into the building walls. The trickling of water obscured the rush of wings until it was too late.

I turned, following the noise. The dark shadow swooped down between the buildings, aiming straight for me.

Drakon!

I tried to lunge out of the way, but I was too slow. He dived low, his shadowy form knocking me to the ground. Though he was transparent smoke, he hit me with the power of a freight train, a combination of electric shock and sonic boom. I slammed down onto my front, ribs aching and breath forced from my lungs.

I nearly lost my grip on my sword and felt the freezing bindings of the black mist. I gripped the hilt tighter, scrambling to my feet. My ribs and knees ached. My insides felt like a prizefighter had beaten up each organ.

I did my best to shake it off, and continued up the street, keeping my gaze alert for Drakon. He was here, somewhere, regrouping and planning a second attack.

He must be able to fly within the freezing mist because he, too, was incorporeal. Or maybe his power was like that of my blade—so strong that it was impervious.

It didn't matter why—only that he was here, and I had to avoid him.

My lungs burned as I ran. I kept my eyes and ears alert. The rush of wings was my only warning. This time, I threw myself to the ground voluntarily. He barely missed me, swooping overhead and hissing his rage.

"Bastard." I surged up, and raced for the top of the street, my breath heaving.

His second attack came without warning, as if he were learning to be quieter. He slammed me to the ground again. I skidded on the stone, pain flaring throughout my whole body. He didn't have the same level of power he'd had in his human form, but his blows were enough to make me feel like I'd been run over by a dump truck.

Aching, I dragged myself to my feet. I was only halfway to the top. The blue glow of the lightning beckoned, but it was so far. All around me, the city was silent and frozen. I waged my own battle in this frozen world, fighting a shadowy dragon that I couldn't hear coming.

Muscles screaming, I ran, half limping. Touching Drakon was like sticking my fingers in a light socket.

The next time, I heard him coming. Just barely, the rush of wings. I was used to listening for Jeff's wings, and I used the skill on Drakon. It would be an attack from the side—from the alley right up ahead on my left.

Maybe he was too excited to land his killing blow, or he was lazy because he knew I couldn't see him coming from the side. Whatever it was, I used it to my advantage.

I raised my sword as I raced toward the alley, meeting him head-on. He flew right at me, level with my head. I dived, plunging up with my blade. The steel sliced at his side, a shallow wound. In his chest, a heart glowed black and bright.

I'd missed. Badly.

But Drakon hissed as steam poured from him. It burned. I shrieked and rolled away. He swept up into the sky.

I scrambled up, clutching my sword tight, and raced for the top of the street, pain engulfing me. Almost there. Just thirty meters to go. I was close enough that I could see the streak of blue lightning.

The sky was brightening as the sun approached the horizon. High above, Drakon swooped overhead. I needed a more direct shot. To his heart.

I sprinted faster. Maybe I could beat him to the lightning.

I was wrong.

He dived right in front of me, then swooped low over the street, hurtling toward me. He flew so low to the ground that he filled the narrow street, giving me nowhere to hide. There were no side streets and no way for me to dodge him. The direct blow could knock me unconscious, and at this angle, reaching his heart was impossible. Beheading was even less likely.

Fear chilled my skin.

Then my eyes caught on a set of stone steps set into the wall on my right. They climbed upward along the building's front face, going toward Drakon. From his angle, he probably couldn't even see that steps were there.

*My only shot.*

I sprinted faster, lungs burning. Drakon was nearly upon me when I leapt onto the steps to my right and raced up them. Drakon slowed, just slightly. He was right under me.

I leapt off the steps, blade plunging downward. I landed on Drakon, the contact shooting pain through every atom. My steel sank into Drakon's back. Not over his heart, but close. He shrieked. The wound was deep, pouring steam. I fell off him, keeping my grip tight on my blade. Agony surged through me from touching him, the prizefighter going for my organs again.

As I crashed to the ground, Drakon swooped upward, going for the sky. His wings faltered.

Jackpot.

I hadn't killed, but I'd done some serious damage.

Gasping and shaking, I dragged myself up, stumbling the last few meters up the street. It opened up into the main courtyard—the center of town.

The blue lightning blazed, brilliant and fierce. It pierced down from the sky, striking the cobblestone ground and holding firm, like a harpoon that kept the cloudy black dome in place.

I ran for it, adrenaline pumping through my veins. The lightning was at least a foot thick, sparking and bright. I wasn't even sure if it *was* lightning, but it crackled with magical energy, making my hair stand on end and burning my eyes.

I squinted, trying to keep my gaze on the magic. There was no time for hesitation. As soon as I neared it, I raised my sword and struck, slicing through the lightning like I was trying to fell a tree.

Electricity blew me off my feet, shooting me backward. I slammed into the ground, losing my grip on my sword. It clattered onto the cobblestones.

I lay on my back, gasping, frozen with electric pain. Above me, the lightning retreated into the sky, disappearing back the way it'd come. If my plan worked, Alton's cage would disappear as well.

Morning light illuminated the dome above me. The gray mist receded, starting at the very top of the dome and disappearing all the way to the ground.

*Hell, yes.*

Now if only I could move, because I had a date with battle.

I groaned as I sat upright, every muscle aching. All around me, people shouted. They were waking up.

Shakily, I stood, then stooped and gathered my sword.

"Phoenix!" My mother's voice sounded from behind me.

I whirled. She raced toward me, her skin pale and hair limp.

Her eyes were wild as she sprinted up to me and threw her arms around me.

"You saved us!" She pulled back and looked at me, pride gleaming in her eyes.

My father ran up to join her. He pulled me in tight for a hug.

"It's not over yet." I pointed toward the mountaintop where Alton had been held captive. It was to be our main battleground. Tension thrummed in my veins, a deep need to be at the battle with my friends. "I have to get over there, quickly. My friends are about to fight the army of the man who did this to you. They need our help."

My mother's gaze sharpened and she nodded, quick to understand the direness of the situation. The panic in my voice probably helped.

She turned and yelled, "Elesius, to arms! The horses!" She looked back at me. "Come, this way!"

She grabbed my hand, and we raced across the courtyard. I forced the pain away, trying to focus on my friends. They needed me.

We ran up to the stables, which were located at the side of the courtyard. Stablehands were readying the mounts, fast and precise.

"That one." My mother pointed to a sleek black horse.

I hurried toward it, lodging my foot in the stirrup and then heaving myself up. My mother launched herself onto her white horse. My father followed suit, climbing atop his gray mount. Around us, citizens of Elesius spilled out of buildings, armed to the teeth. Cavalry leapt upon horses, others ran on foot, gathering in the square.

"We go to Darktop Mountain!" my mother called. She looked at me and murmured, "Who the hell are we fighting?"

"Demons. Kill only the demons." I didn't want my friends getting caught in the crossfire.

My mother nodded, gaze firm, then turned back to the crowd.

"We wage war against the demons who imprisoned us! Slay all those with horns."

Yeah, that worked.

My mother turned to me. "We ride."

Then she turned her mount and galloped off up the street. I directed my horse after her, following as she rode expertly towards the edge of the dome, where I presumed there was a shortcut.

Jeez, she was a badass.

My father followed behind me, the rest of the army racing along behind him. The road gave way to a section of mountain ridge. Two hundred meters in the distance, the white barrier shimmered. I followed my mother, guiding my mount around boulders.

We plowed through the shimmering white veil, spilling out onto the other side. In the distance, at the top of the ridge, the blue lightning cage was gone. We were just in time.

My friends dropped from their hiding places in the trees, racing for Alton, who stood bound next to the glittering black orb. Del threw her icicle bolts while Ares raced ahead with his shadow sword. Roarke took to the sky, no doubt planning to do some beheading.

The demons that'd been guarding the cage surged to their feet, roaring the alarm. There would be more. Overhead, Drakon swooped through the sky. Was he recovered from the wound I'd delivered?

I pressed my fingertips to my comms charm. "Cass! Come get me!"

My mother turned back to look at me. I pointed toward the demons. "The fight is there. Mine is in the sky."

"Be safe." Her voice was fierce. She looked past me, at the army that had followed. "This way!"

She galloped off, leading the charge. The army surged by me.

Cass plunged down from the sky, already in her griffon form.

I leapt off my mount, then scrambled onto her back. Her magic glowed bright and strong as she soared into the sky, golden wings carrying us high.

As planned, she raced for Drakon, who wheeled high overhead, recovering from my attack and no doubt waiting to strike. The sun had now crested the horizon, making it easy to see him. Our goal was to distract him while the army on the ground rescued Alton and the mysterious black orb.

"Hey, Drakon!" I screamed.

He whirled toward us. I could feel his rage, vibrating on the air. He charged. Cass spun and raced away, leading him from the fight. Though my blade could hurt him, I was going to have to be careful about how I wielded it. One touch from him could shock us out of the sky.

In that moment, Jeff arrived. He was huge again, no doubt having recouped his magic. The Pūķi appeared at his side.

*Shit.*

*Please be careful, guys.*

They swooped and dived, trying to distract Drakon. They were good at keeping out of his reach, but he was more intent on reaching us. If he turned on them...

"Try to come up on him from underneath!" I called to Cass.

She dived low, flying under Drakon. She was smaller and faster than him, and we shot upward toward his belly. I leaned up as far as I could, stretching my sword arm.

We were nearly to him when I shouted, "Now!"

I sliced with my blade as she dodged away. The tip of the steel gouged his belly, but Cass's wing clipped his. She shuddered and tumbled in the air as the electric shock tore through her. I clung to her back, trying not to fall as my skin turned to ice and my heart leapt into my thorax.

The ground was so far below. We tumbled toward it through the air, the shock too much for Cass. We were only one hundred meters above when she managed to right herself, hurtling up through the sky on shaky wings.

Above, Drakon hovered. Jeff and the Pūķis darted around him. I'd wounded him, but not badly. And it was impossible to strike from Cass's back.

Below, the battle raged. My mother's army fought alongside my friends, wielding weapons and magic. They seemed evenly matched in numbers, but I didn't have time to study them.

I searched for Drakon. He was still hovering on the air, perhaps recovering from my blow or debating whether to go after the army or me.

I needed a new plan. My mind raced. In the distance, Aidan attacked demons in his griffon form. A thought blazed.

"Jeff!" I cried. "Get Aidan! The griffon!"

Cass stiffened beneath me. Fortunately, Jeff was fast, darting toward Aidan like the wind. Aidan was even faster, at my side in a moment.

"Go below Drakon," I shouted to him. "Cass, you go above! Jeff, you distract him."

Cass shrieked, a sound of pure griffon rage. She clearly knew what I planned and didn't like it. Frankly, I didn't like it either. But I could see no other way.

"Do it!" I screamed. "Unless you've got a better plan! Which you don't."

She hissed, another noise I'd never heard her make, then flew toward Drakon, coming up from behind him to hover on top. He'd clearly shaken off the effects of my first blow, because he was going after Jeff, who'd just blown fire in his eyes. Aidan hovered below.

This was it.

"Get lower!" I said.

Cass flew lower, diving for Drakon. When she was only five feet above, I didn't hesitate. I leapt off her back.

I plummeted toward Drakon, my sword pointed downward

and aiming for his glowing black heart. Cass flew away, avoiding his electrical charge. It slammed into me, shooting pain to the marrow of my bones.

One thought flashed through my mind: *Don't let go of the sword.*

My blade plunged into his back, close to his heart. The pain made it nearly impossible to see, so I had no idea if I had struck true, but he roared and shook me off. *At least I hit something*, I thought as I fell off his back. Probably not his heart, but the wound was grievous. Through bleary vision, I saw him tumbling through the sky, thrashing from my blow.

*Please catch me, Aidan.*

The wind whipped past me as I fell, in too much shock to feel the pain anymore. I struggled, trying to see where I was going. I caught sight of a golden blur, then slammed into it.

I grabbed tight, holding to whatever I could. I nearly dropped my blade, but managed to hold on to it as I clung with my legs and gripped the base of a wing with my free hand.

We were near the ground, right over the battle. I tried to grip Aidan tight, almost too weak to hold on. My gaze zeroed in on Ares, who fought like a man possessed, beheading demon after demon.

We were only fifteen feet above the battle and heading down fast. My grip was so weak now that I was going to slide off at any moment. As if he felt my gaze, Ares looked up. His eyes landed on mine.

I fell, losing my grip on Aidan. My stomach fell and my skin chilled.

Ares caught me, going to his knees with an "Oof."

Up above, Drakon shrieked. Around us, the battle stilled. The demons turned tail and ran. I'd wounded Drakon enough to drive him off. I grinned. Most of my body felt numb, but I could feel the smile.

"We need to stop meeting like this," Ares said.

"I don't mind." Shaking, I tried to stand. Limp noodles were firm compared to me.

Ares had to help me to my feet, keeping an arm wrapped around my waist. "What happened to you?" he asked.

"Electric shocks? Sonic booms? I'm not sure. Whatever it is, Drakon is basically poisonous to the touch."

He kissed me on the head. I surveyed the battle, trying to take my mind off the pain that suffused every inch of me.

Around us, our allies tended to the wounded. My frantic gaze found all of my friends. Not all looked great—Roarke had a bad limp and Connor's face was covered in blood, among other injuries—but all were standing. My mother was still mounted on her white horse. She and the horse were spattered in blood. The same for my father.

Bree and Ana were looting the corpses of the dead demons. Looking for transportation charms, I'd bet. At least, that was what I'd be doing.

Cass landed, galloping toward me. Even in her griffon form, she looked pissed. In a blur of golden light, she shifted.

"What the hell were you thinking?" she shouted.

"I don't know." I grinned shakily, relieved just to be alive. "In hindsight, it was pretty dumb."

Ares looked down at me. "What did you do?"

"You didn't see?" Cass's face turned bright red. "She jumped off my back, tried to stab a dragon, and planned to land on Aidan's back."

Ares grimaced. "That was...risky. Brave, but risky."

"Yeah. I won't do it again." My limbs started to shake, as if my body had just caught up to the stupidity of what my brain had made me do. My knees felt like Jello. "Can we go home? I think I need to puke."

# CHAPTER FIFTEEN

The next evening, everyone was supposed to meet at P & P. Connor shut the whole place down for the day. First, so that he and Claire could recover from their wounds, and second, so that I could thank everyone who had fought. Though the whole town of Elesius couldn't attend, my mother and father managed.

We all walked toward the coffee shop together, along with Ares. The moon was full overhead, and the golden streetlamp illuminated the sidewalk.

"Did you lose many people?" I asked my mother. We hadn't been able to talk after the battle because everyone had needed their wounds tended to, and I'd been worried.

"Only four," my mother said.

My heart ached. If only I'd been faster. "I'm sorry."

"Don't be. We know our duty."

"That's very stoic."

She stopped, grabbing my arm so that I halted next to her, and smiled at me. "We're stoic for a valuable cause. You performed admirably. You are truly worthy of your role, Phoenix." Before I could thank her, she scowled. "But don't go leaping through the air like that again."

"I promise. I won't. I really wasn't a fan." A laugh escaped me, and I met Ares's eyes. He smiled, no doubt remembering that I'd puked as I'd said I would. "I don't think heights are for me."

"You're a risk taker, Phoenix. It's necessary when one has a role such as yours to perform. But be careful." She hugged me. "We don't want to lose you."

I hugged her back, then hugged my father, who kissed the top of my head. Just being around my parents filled me with joy.

"Come on," I said. "The party has started."

We continued down the street, entering the cozy warmth of P & P to the sound of Connor's music. Everyone was here, though most people sported bandages or braces. I still felt a little crappy myself, like I was one giant bruise that needed time to heal.

Ares pressed a kiss to my forehead. "Let me get you a drink. The usual?"

I smiled up at him. "You know me so well."

He went to get me a bourbon, and I found Cass and Del in the middle of the room.

"Hey!" Del wrapped an arm around me and squeezed. "How are you?"

"Good. You?"

"All right. Healed up."

"Same." Cass smiled.

"Good." I checked out the crowd.

The FireSouls were all here, but they weren't dressed in their usual armor, thank fates. I didn't want to see armor or weapons for at least twenty-four hours. Aerdeca and Mordaca wore their usual white and black outfits, while Bree and Ana wore their *Mad Max* attire like they were ready to jump back into battle at any moment. Even Jeff was over in the corner, back to his normal, small size.

Ares joined us, handing me my glass of Four Roses.

"You're a hero," I said.

"You too," Del said. "Super brave, jumping off of Cass like that."

Cass caught my eye. "Yeah, brave. But also an idiot." She punched me lightly on the shoulder. "But you're my kind of idiot."

I laughed, then clinked my glass with her can of PBR. Del lifted her mug of boxed wine, tapping her glass to ours.

"I'm going to go say thank you to everyone," I said. "Then we should meet with Alton to see what he has to say about Drakon."

Cass nodded. "Good plan."

I made my way into the crowd, stopping to thank everyone who'd fought at our side. The sight of their injuries made me wince, and the thought of the dead made me tear up, but I was so grateful for their help. I never could have done this alone.

I finished at the group of FireSouls, all of whom sat around Alton in the corner. The wound at his cheek was now a dashing scar.

He smiled. "Thanks for what you did back there."

"Anytime."

Ares joined me, and I reached for his hand. Cass and Del came to stand at our sides, along with Aidan and Roarke.

"Is there a chance you overheard anything from Drakon or his men?" I asked.

He grinned. "Didn't hear anything. He was too smart to talk around me. But he abducted the wrong FireSoul."

My heart beat faster. This was going to be good. I could just tell. "How so?"

"I'm a mind reader."

"Oh, snap," Del whispered.

"So you know that he wants to steal all the power from the last remaining dragons," I said.

He nodded. "He was testing a spell that would help him do that. He'd never used it before and wanted to test it on people.

He'd hoped to capture you as well, but I don't think he expected you to go into the city. That upset his plan."

"He didn't realize I had a blade that would get me in."

Alton shook his head. "He didn't. Nor did he realize the blade could wound him. It saved your life." He looked at Del and Cass. "And theirs. And mine."

"So, we rescued you and saved the black orb, which is now locked up safely in the Vampire Realm, being studied by their smartest scholars. Does that mean he can't deploy his spell against the dragons?" I phrased it as a question because it sounded too good to be true.

Alton frowned. "No. Unfortunately not. He proved his spell worked. Now he just needs to get another magical battery like the black gem."

"Damn it." I'd been expecting that—this wasn't nearly over yet —but it still sucked. "Does he have another battery?"

"Not yet, but soon. There's one other that he is trying to get, but he didn't think about it in much detail. I'm not sure what it is, but I don't think he has it quite yet."

"But he's on the path to finding it?" I asked.

"Yes." Alton nodded. "And he'll also hunt other FireSouls. He'll need more of us to steal the power from the dragons."

"So FireSouls have to be on the alert," Ares said. "Keep to your realm where he can't get to you. We'll protect the ones on Earth."

"There are more than we know about," Cass said. "Not just us."

"But he wants us for the final spell," I said. "He may not threaten the others."

"Then we'll have to be careful," Del said.

"We'll help you," Alton said. "However you need."

Mordaca and Aerdeca joined us, coming to stand next to Corin and Fiona.

"You know we're in," Mordaca said.

"We can help, too," Bree said.

Ana nodded.

My mother, who stood behind Bree, just smiled. I smiled back, knowing she'd be there for us. As would my father. Ares squeezed my hand.

My heart thumped in my chest. Everyone here was in this together. Despite the danger and the risk, they'd be there when I needed them. And I was going to need them. What we were facing... It was bigger than all of us alone. It didn't matter if I was ready to fight what was coming, because it was coming whether I was ready or not. We may have beaten Drakon today, but there was a bigger fight waiting on the horizon tomorrow.

# EPILOGUE

The forest was quiet when I arrived at the outskirts of Elesius. With Drakon's spell broken, I could now enter at will without slamming into a wall.

I'd come alone, desperate to find the forest spirit who had helped me. The woods were quiet, as usual. Without life, there wasn't much to make sound. Just the dead trees keeping vigil.

"Hello?" I called.

There was no response. I started walking, running my fingertips over the bark of the trees as I passed. The death in this place still made me cringe. I'd never get used to it.

Jeff appeared next to me. He was still small, and he blew fire happily from his nose.

"Not here!" I said. "This place is just kindling."

"That it is." The voice came from behind me.

I turned. The forest spirit stood there, looking just as she had before. Beautiful and serene, wearing the same long, white dress. I seriously doubted that her wardrobe was of much concern to her. She drifted toward me.

Up close, the leaves that made up her hair looked delicate and fine.

"You're the ghost of this forest, aren't you?" I asked.

She inclined her head. "I am."

"But you weren't always a ghost. You looked more solid in my dream."

"I've always been a spirit. But as the forest has died, I've faded."

"You mean, as I've sucked the life out of you."

She smiled. I should've felt malevolence coming from her, considering that I'd killed her. But I felt nothing of the sort. Just calm acceptance. "This was my fate."

"I don't want it to be your fate. I don't want Elesius to die because of me. I don't want *you* to die because of me." My heart twisted.

Jeff blew fire, clearly disconcerted.

There had to be *something* I could do. I had to try.

I reached for her, slowing my hand as it neared her shoulder. She looked at me, brows raised. But she didn't stop me, so I touched her shoulder.

She felt dark—if it were possible for someone to feel that way, at least. I didn't know what it was, precisely, but it sucked.

I tried feeding some of my magic into her. It flowed slowly, in fits and starts.

"Don't!" She pushed me back. "You need your magic."

"It's not finite." I looked at Jeff. "Especially now that I have him. I'll regenerate it."

"You *need* it."

"Let me just try to give you a little." I reached out and touched Jeff. Warmth and power flowed into me. "See? He's helping." I had no idea the extent of the little dragon's magic, but it was definitely helping.

She frowned, studying us. Finally, she nodded.

I touched her shoulder again, this time feeding her more of my power. Jeff helped, making it flow faster and fuller. Her cheeks began to glow. She smiled.

Then she pulled back, panting. "That's enough."

Around me, the trees trembled. My heart thudded. I braced myself.

Tiny green shoots of grass poked up through the forest floor. They were sparse and thin, but they were definitely there.

I gasped. "Do you see that?"

The forest spirit stared with wide eyes. She looked up at me. "You are magnificent."

I blushed, then looked back at the grass. It waved in the slight breeze, a beautiful bright green. Hope flared in my chest. Elesius was coming back to life.

~~~

Nix's last book will be out in late September. If you haven't had a chance to read *Hidden Magic*, the Dragon's Gift series starter, you can get it for free by signing up for my newsletter at Visit www.linseyhall.com/subscribe. Turn the page for an excerpt.

# THANK YOU FOR READING!

I hope you enjoyed reading this book as much as I enjoyed writing it. Reviews are *so* helpful to authors. I really appreciate all reviews, both positive and negative. If you want to leave one, you can do so on Amazon.

Turn the page for an excerpt of *Hidden Magic*, which you can get for free by signing up for my mailing list at www.linseyhall.com/subscribe.

# EXCERPT OF HIDDEN MAGIC

*(Told from the perspective of Cass Clereaux)*

*Jungle, Southeast Asia*
*Five years before the events in Demon Magic*

"How much are we being paid for this job again?" I asked as I glanced at the inhabitants filling the bar. It was a motley crowd of supernaturals, many of whom looked shifty as hell.

"Not nearly enough." Del frowned at the man across the bar, who was giving her his best sexy face. There was a lot of eyebrow movement happening. "Is he having a seizure?"

"Looks like it." Nix grinned. "Though I gotta say, I wasn't expecting this. We're basically in a tree, for magic's sake. In the middle of the jungle! Where are all these dudes coming from?"

"According to my info, there's a mining operation near here. Though I'd say we're more *under* a tree than *in* a tree."

"I'm with Cass," Del said. "Under, not in."

"Fair enough." Nix's green eyes traveled around the room.

We were deep in Southeast Asia, in a bar that had long ago

been reclaimed by the jungle. A massive fig tree had grown over and around the ancient building, its huge roots encapsulating the stone walls. It was straight out of a fairy tale. Monks had once lived here, but a few supernaturals of indeterminate species had gotten ahold of it and turned it into a watering hole for the local supernaturals. We were meeting our local contact here, but he was late.

"Hey, pretty lady." A smarmy voice sounded from my left. "What are you?"

I turned to face the guy who was giving me the up and down, his gaze roving from my tank top to my shorts. He wasn't Clarence, our local contact. And if he meant "what kind of supernatural are you?" I sure as hell wouldn't be answering.

"Not interested is what I am," I said.

"Aww, that's no way to treat a guy." He grasped my hip, rubbing his thumb up and down.

I gagged, then smacked his hand away, tempted to throat-punch him. It was a favorite move of mine, but I didn't want to start a fight before Clarence got here. Didn't want to piss off the boss and all. He liked it when jobs went smoothly.

The man raised his hands. "Hey, hey. No need to get feisty. You three sisters?"

I glanced doubtfully at Nix and Del, with their dark hair that was so different from my red. We might call ourselves sisters—*deirfiúr* in our native Irish—but this idiot didn't know that. We were all about twenty years old, but we looked nothing alike.

"Go away," I said. I had no patience for dudes who touched me within a second of saying hello. "Run along and flirt with your hand, because that's all the action you'll be getting tonight."

His face turned a mottled red, and he raised a fist. His magic welled, the scent of rotten fruit overwhelming.

He thought he was going to smack me? Or use his magic against me?

I lashed out, punching him in the throat as I'd wanted to

earlier. His eyes bulged and he gagged. I kneed him in the crotch, grinning when he keeled over.

"Hey!" A burly man with a beard lunged for us, his buddy beside him following. "That's no way—"

"To treat a guy?" I finished for him as I kicked out at him. My tall, heavy boots collided with his chest, sending him flying backward. I might not use my magic, but I sure as hell could fight.

His friend raised his hand and sent a blast of wind at us. It threw me backward, sending me skidding across the floor.

By the time I'd scrambled to my feet, a brawl had broken out in the bar. Fists flew left and right, with a bit of magic thrown in. Nothing bad enough to ruin the bar, like jets of flame, because no one wanted to destroy the only watering hole for a hundred miles, but enough that it lit up the air with varying magical signatures.

Nix conjured a baseball bat and swung it at a guy who charged her, while Del teleported behind a man and smashed a chair over his head. I'd always been jealous of Del's ability to sneak up on people like that.

All in all, it was turning into a good evening. Watching a fight between supernaturals was fun.

"Enough!" the bartender bellowed, right before I could throw myself back into the fray. "Or no more beer!"

The bar settled down immediately. I glared at the jerk who'd started it. There was no way I'd take the blame, even though I'd thrown the first punch. He should have known better.

The bartender gave me a look and I shrugged, hiking a thumb at the jerk who'd touched me. "He shoulda kept his hands to himself."

"Fair enough," the bartender said.

I nodded and turned to find Nix and Del. They'd grabbed our beers and were putting them on a table in the corner. I went to join them.

We were a team. Sisters by choice, ever since we'd woken in a field at fifteen with no memories other than those that said we were FireSouls on the run from someone who had hurt us. Who was hunting us.

Our biggest goal, even bigger than getting out from under our current boss's thumb, was to save enough money to buy concealment charms that would hide us from the monster who hunted us. He was just a shadowy memory, but it was enough to keep us running.

"Where is Clarence, anyway?" I pulled my damp tank top away from my sweaty skin. The jungle was damned hot. We couldn't break into the temple until Clarence gave us the information we needed to get past the guard at the front. And we didn't need to spend too much longer in this bar.

Del glanced at her watch, her blue eyes flashing with annoyance. "He's twenty minutes late. Old Man Bastard said he should be here at eight."

Old Man Bastard—OMB for short—was our boss. His name said it all. Del, Nix, and I were FireSouls, the most despised species of supernatural because we could steal other magical being's powers if we killed them. We'd never done that, of course, but OMB didn't care. He'd figured out our secret when we were too young to hide it effectively and had been blackmailing us to work for him ever since.

It'd been four years of finding and stealing treasure on his behalf. Treasure hunting was our other talent, a gift from the dragon with whom legend said we shared a soul. No one had seen a dragon in centuries, so I wasn't sure if the legend was even true, but dragons were covetous, so it made sense they had a knack for finding treasure.

"What are we after again?" Nix asked.

"A pair of obsidian daggers," Del said. "Nice ones."

"And how much is this job worth?" Nix repeated my earlier question. Money was always on our minds. It was our only chance at buying our freedom, but OMB didn't pay us enough for it to be feasible anytime soon. We kept meticulous track of our earnings and saved like misers anyway.

"A thousand each."

"Damn, that's pathetic." I slouched back in my chair and stared up at the ceiling, too bummed about our crappy pay to even be impressed by the stonework and vines above my head.

"Hey, pretty ladies." The oily voice made my skin crawl. We could just not get a break in here. I looked up to see Clarence, our contact.

Clarence was a tall man, slender as a vine, and had the slicked back hair and pencil-thin mustache of a 1940s movie star. Unfortunately, it didn't work on him. Probably because his stare was like a lizard's. He was more Gomez Addams than Clark Gable. I'd bet anything that he liked working for OMB.

"Hey, Clarence," I said. "Pull up a seat and tell us how to get into the temple."

Clarence slid into a chair, his movement eerily snakelike. I shivered and scooted my chair away, bumping into Del. The scent of her magic flared, a clean hit of fresh laundry, as she no doubt suppressed her instinct to transport away from Clarence. If I had her gift of teleportation, I'd have to repress it as well.

"How about a drink first?" Clarence said.

Del growled, but Nix interjected, her voice almost nice. She had the most self control out of the three of us. "No can do, Clarence. You know... Mr. Oribis"—her voice tripped on the name, probably because she wanted to call him OMB—"wants the daggers soon. Maybe next time, though."

"Next time." Clarence shook his head like he didn't believe her. He might be a snake, but he was a clever one. His chest puffed up a bit. "You know I'm the only one who knows how to get into the temple. How to get into any of the places in this jungle."

"And we're so grateful you're meeting with us. Mr. Oribis is so grateful." Nix dug into her pocket and pulled out the crumpled envelope that contained Clarence's pay. We'd counted it and found—unsurprisingly—that it was more than ours combined, even though all he had to do was chat with us for two minutes. I'd wanted to scream when I'd seen it.

Clarence's gaze snapped to the money. "All right, all right."

Apparently his need to be flattered went out the window when cash was in front of his face. Couldn't blame him, though. I was the same way.

"So, what are we up against?" I asked.

The temple containing the daggers had been built by supernaturals over a thousand years ago. Like other temples of its kind, it was magically protected. Clarence's intel would save us a ton of time and damage to the temple if we could get around the enchantments rather than breaking through them.

"Dvarapala. A big one."

"A gatekeeper?" I'd seen one of the giant, stone monster statues at another temple before.

"Yep." He nodded slowly. "Impossible to get through. The temple's as big as the Titanic—hidden from humans, of course—but no one's been inside in centuries, they say."

Hidden from humans was a given. They had no idea supernaturals existed, and we wanted to keep it that way.

"So how'd you figure out the way in?" Del asked. "And why *haven't* you gone in? Bet there's lots of stuff you could fence in there. Temples are usually full of treasure."

"A bit of pertinent research told me how to get in. And I'd rather sell the entrance information and save my hide. It won't be easy to get past the booby traps in there."

Hide? Snakeskin, more like. Though he had a point. I didn't think he'd last long trying to get through a temple on his own.

"So? Spill it," I said, anxious to get going.

He leaned in, and the overpowering scent of cologne and sweat hit me. I grimaced, held my breath, then leaned forward to hear his whispers.

\*\*\*

As soon as Clarence walked away, the communications charms around my neck vibrated. I jumped, then groaned. Only one person had access to this charm.

I shoved the small package Clarence had given me into my short's pocket and pressed my fingertips to the comms charm, igniting its magic.

"Hello, Mr. Oribis." I swallowed my bile at having to be polite.

"Girls," he grumbled.

Nix made a gagging face. We hated when he called us girls.

"Change of plans. You need to go to the temple tonight."

"What? But it's dark. We're going tomorrow." He never changed the plans on us. This was weird.

"I need the daggers sooner. Go tonight."

My mind raced. "The jungle is more dangerous in the dark. We'll do it if you pay us more."

"Twice the usual," Del said.

A tinny laugh echoed from the charm. "Pay *you* more? You're lucky I pay you at all."

I gritted my teeth and said, "But we've been working for you for four years without a raise."

"And you'll be working for me for four more years. And four after that. And four after that." Annoyance lurked in his tone. So did his low opinion of us.

Del's and Nix's brows crinkled in distress. We'd always suspected that OMB wasn't planning to let us buy our freedom, but he'd dangled that carrot in front of us. What he'd just said made that seem like a big fat lie, though. One we could add to the many others he'd told us.

An urge to rebel, to stand up to the bully who controlled our lives, seethed in my chest.

"No," I said. "You treat us like crap, and I'm sick of it. Pay us fairly."

"I treat you like *crap,* as you so eloquently put it, because that is exactly what you are. *FireSouls.*" He spit the last word, imbuing it with so much venom I thought it might poison me.

I flinched, frantically glancing around to see if anyone in the bar had heard what he'd called us. Fortunately, they were all distracted. That didn't stop my heart from thundering in my ears as rage replaced the fear. I opened my mouth to shout at him, but snapped it shut. I was too afraid of pissing him off.

"Get it by dawn," he barked. "Or I'm turning one of you in to the Order of the Magica. Prison will be the least of your worries. They might just execute you."

I gasped. "You wouldn't." Our government hunted and imprisoned—or destroyed—FireSouls.

"Oh, I would. And I'd enjoy it. The three of you have been more trouble than you're worth. You're getting cocky, thinking you have a say in things like this. Get the daggers by dawn, or one of you ends up in the hands of the Order."

My skin chilled, and the floor felt like it had dropped out from under me. He was serious.

"Fine." I bit off the end of the word, barely keeping my voice from shaking. "We'll do it tonight. Del will transport them to you as soon as we have them."

"Excellent." Satisfaction rang in his tone, and my skin crawled. "Don't disappoint me, or you know what will happen."

The magic in the charm died. He'd broken the connection.

I collapsed back against the chair. In times like these, I wished I had it in me to kill. Sure, I offed demons when they came at me on our jobs, but that was easy because they didn't actually die. Killing their earthly bodies just sent them back to their hell.

But I couldn't kill another supernatural. Not even OMB. It might get us out of this lifetime of servitude, but I didn't have it in me. And what if I failed? I was too afraid of his rage—and the consequences—if I didn't succeed.

"Shit, shit, shit." Nix's green eyes were stark in her pale face. "He means it."

"Yeah." Del's voice shook. "We need to get those daggers."

"Now," I said.

"I wish I could just conjure a forgery," Nix said. "I really don't want to go out into the jungle tonight. Getting past the Dvarapala in the dark will suck."

Nix was a conjurer, able to create almost anything using just her magic. Massive or complex things, like airplanes or guns, were outside of her ability, but a couple of daggers wouldn't be hard.

Trouble was, they were a magical artifact, enchanted with the ability to return to whoever had thrown them. Like boomerangs. Though Nix could conjure the daggers, we couldn't enchant them.

"We need to go. We only have six hours until dawn." I grabbed my short swords from the table and stood, shoving them into the holsters strapped to my back.

A hush descended over the crowded bar.

I stiffened, but the sound of the staticky TV in the corner made me relax. They weren't interested in me. Just the news, which was probably being routed through a dozen techno-witches to get this far into the jungle.

The grave voice of the female reporter echoed through the quiet bar. "The FireSoul was apprehended outside of his apartment in Magic's Bend, Oregon. He is currently in the custody of the Order of the Magica, and his trial is scheduled for tomorrow morning. My sources report that execution is possible."

I stifled a crazed laugh. Perfect timing. Just what we needed to hear after OMB's threat. A reminder of what would happen if he turned us into the Order of the Magica. The hush that had descended over the previously rowdy crowd—the kind of hush you get at the scene of a big accident—indicated what an interesting freaking topic this was. FireSouls were the bogeymen. *I* was the bogeyman, even though I didn't use my powers. But as long as no one found out, we were safe.

My gaze darted to Del and Nix. They nodded toward the door. It was definitely time to go.

As the newscaster turned her report toward something more boring and the crowd got rowdy again, we threaded our way between the tiny tables and chairs.

I shoved the heavy wooden door open and sucked in a breath of sticky jungle air, relieved to be out of the bar. Night creatures screeched, and moonlight filtered through the trees above. The jungle would be a nice place if it weren't full of things that wanted to kill us.

"We're never escaping him, are we?" Nix said softly.

"We will." Somehow. Someday. "Let's just deal with this for now."

We found our motorcycles, which were parked in the lot with a dozen other identical ones. They were hulking beasts with massive, all-terrain tires meant for the jungle floor. We'd done a lot of work in Southeast Asia this year, and these were our favored forms of transportation in this part of the world.

Del could transport us, but it was better if she saved her power. It wasn't infinite, though it did regenerate. But we'd learned a long time ago to save Del's power for our escape. Nothing worse than being trapped in a temple with pissed off guardians and a few tripped booby traps.

We'd scouted out the location of the temple earlier that day, so we knew where to go.

I swung my leg over Secretariat—I liked to name my vehicles —and kicked the clutch. The engine roared to life. Nix and Del followed, and we peeled out of the lot, leaving the dingy yellow light of the bar behind.

Our headlights illuminated the dirt road as we sped through the night. Huge fig trees dotted the path on either side, their twisted trunks and roots forming an eerie corridor. Elephant-ear sized leaves swayed in the wind, a dark emerald that gleamed in the light.

Jungle animals howled, and enormous lightning bugs flitted along the path. They were too big to be regular bugs, so they were most likely some kind of fairy, but I wasn't going to stop to investigate. There were dangerous creatures in the jungle at night —one of the reasons we hadn't wanted to go now—and in our world, fairies could be considered dangerous.

Especially if you called them lightning bugs.

A roar sounded in the distance, echoing through the jungle and making the leaves rustle on either side as small animals scurried for safety.

The roar came again, only closer.

Then another, and another.

"Oh shit," I muttered. This was bad.

~~~

Visit www.linseyhall.com/subscribe and subscribe to my mailing list to get the rest of Hidden Magic for free.

# AUTHOR'S NOTE

Thank you so much for reading *Origin of Magic!* If you've read any of my other books, you won't be surprised to hear that I included historical elements. If you're interested in learning more about that, read on. At the end, I'll talk a bit about why Nix and her *deirfiúr* are treasure hunters and how I try to make that fit with archaeology's ethics (which don't condone treasure hunting, as I'm sure you might have guessed).

*Enemy of Magic* had several historical and mythological influences. The riddle the Ares and Nix are asked to solve in the vampire realm is one of the riddles from the Exeter book. Written in the 11th century, the Exeter book is a collection of poetry and riddles written by the Anglo-Saxons. The answers to the riddle aren't included in the book, but scholars have given it their best shot to identify them.

Norse mythology and history play a heavy role in the later half of the book. The *dvergr*, the light fey and the dark fey, and the Jötunn are all borrowed directly from Norse mythology. As was Draugen, a water monster who is the ghost of a man who died at sea. When he appears, he gives a terrible scream before attempting to drown fishermen and sailors. Jörmungand is an important piece of Norse mythology. He is the World Serpent, the offspring of a giantess name Angerboda and Loki. He lays beneath the world, his body so long that he encircles the planet beneath the ocean. I invented his winged children, however.

Sven the Viking, who was buried with his boat and treasure, was based off the Oseberg ship found in Norway in the early 20th century. Vikings would often bury their most powerful in beautiful boats filled with treasure. Several of these boats have been found by archaeologists, some in incredible states of preservation. The battle that Sven the Viking sailed them towards was based on the Viking battle of Fimreite that took place in the Sognefjord, in Western Norway. The battle was fought on the 15th of June, 1184 and led to Sverre Sigurdsson taking the Norwegian throne from Magnus Erlingsson. During a Viking naval battle, ships would often attempt to ram each other, or the men would fight with longbows and spears when they were close enough to reach.

That's it for the historical influences in *Enemy of Magic*. However, one of the most important things about this book is how Nix and her *deirfiúr* treat artifacts and their business, Ancient Magic.

As I'm sure you know, archaeology isn't quite like Indiana Jones (for which I'm both grateful and bitterly disappointed). Sure, it's exciting and full of travel. However, booby-traps are not as common as I expected. Total number of booby-traps I have encountered in my career: zero. Still hoping, though.

When I chose to write a series about archaeology and treasure hunting, I knew I had a careful line to tread. There is a big difference between these two activities. As much as I value artifacts, they are not treasure. Not even the gold artifacts. They are pieces of our history that contain valuable information, and as such, they belong to all of us. Every artifact that is excavated should be properly conserved and stored in a museum so that everyone can have access to our history. No one single person can own history, and I believe very strongly that individuals should not own artifacts. Treasure hunting is the pursuit of artifacts for personal gain.

So why did I make Nix and her *deirfiúr* treasure hunters? I'd have loved to call them archaeologists, but nothing about their work is like archaeology. Archaeology is a very laborious, painstaking process—and it certainly doesn't involve selling artifacts. That wouldn't work for the fast-paced, adventurous series that I had planned for *Dragon's Gift*. Not to mention the fact that dragons are famous for coveting treasure. Considering where the *deirfiúr* got their skills from, it just made sense to call them treasure hunters.

Even though I write urban fantasy, I strive for accuracy. The *deirfiúr* don't engage in archaeological practices—therefore, I cannot call them archaeologists. I also have a duty as an archaeologist to properly represent my field and our goals—namely, to protect and share history. Treasure hunting doesn't do this. One of the biggest battles that archaeology faces today is protecting cultural heritage from thieves.

I debated long and hard about not only what to call the heroines of this series, but also about how they would do their jobs. I wanted it to involve all the cool things we think about when we think about archaeology—namely, the Indiana Jones stuff, whether it's real or not. But I didn't know quite how to do that while still staying within the bounds of my own ethics. I can cut myself and other writers some slack because this is fiction, but I couldn't go too far into smash and grab treasure hunting.

I consulted some of my archaeology colleagues to get their take, which was immensely helpful. Wayne Lusardi, the State Maritime Archaeologist for Michigan, and Douglas Inglis and Veronica Morris, both archaeologists for Interactive Heritage, were immensely helpful with ideas. My biggest problem was figuring out how to have the heroines steal artifacts from tombs and then sell them and still sleep at night. Everything I've just said is pretty counter to this, right?

That's where the magic comes in. The heroines aren't after the artifacts themselves (they put them back where they found them, if you recall)—they're after the magic that the artifacts contain. They're more like magic hunters than treasure hunters. That solved a big part of my problem. At least they were putting the artifacts back. Though that's not proper archaeology, I could let it pass. At least it's clear that they believe they shouldn't keep the artifact or harm the site. But the SuperNerd in me said, "Well, that magic is part of the artifact's context. It's important to the artifact and shouldn't be removed and sold."

Now *that* was a problem. I couldn't escape my SuperNerd self, so I was in a real conundrum. Fortunately, that's where the immensely intelligent Wayne Lusardi came in. He suggested that the magic could have an expiration date. If the magic wasn't used before it decayed, it could cause huge problems. Think explosions and tornado spells run amok. It could ruin the entire site, not to mention possibly cause injury and death. That would be very bad.

So now you see why Nix and her *deirfiúr* don't just steal artifacts to sell them. Not only is selling the magic cooler, it's also better from an ethical standpoint, especially if the magic was going to cause problems in the long run. These aren't perfect solutions—the perfect solution would be sending in a team of archaeologists to carefully record the site and remove the dangerous magic—but that wouldn't be a very fun book.

Thanks again for reading (especially if you got this far!). I hope you enjoyed the story and will stick with Nix on the rest of her adventure!

# ACKNOWLEDGMENTS

Thank you, Ben, for everything. There would be no books without you.

Thank you to Jena O'Connor and Adam at Fine Point Publishing for your excellent editing. The book is immensely better because of you both! Thank you to Orina Kafe for the beautiful cover art. Thank you to Jim O'Keefe for the band recommendation of Ghoston Road. Thank you to Aisha Panjwaneey, Jessica Crosby, Richard A. Goodrum, and Vicki C. Jones for your keen eyes in spotting errors.

The Dragon's Gift series is a product of my two lives: one as an archaeologist and one as a novelist. Combining these two took a bit of work. I'd like to thank my friends, Wayne Lusardi, the State Maritime Archaeologist for Michigan, and Douglas Inglis and Veronica Morris, both archaeologists for Interactive Heritage, for their ideas about how to have a treasure hunter heroine that doesn't conflict too much with archaeology's ethics. The Author's Note contains a bit more about this if you are interested.

# GLOSSARY

Alpha Council - There are two governments that enforce law for supernaturals—the Alpha Council and the Order of the Magica. The Alpha Council governs all shifters. They work cooperatively with the Alpha Council when necessary—for example, when capturing FireSouls.

Blood Sorceress - A type of Magica who can create magic using blood.

Conjurer - A Magica who uses magic to create something from nothing. They cannot create magic, but if there is magic around them, they can put that magic into their conjuration.

Dark Magic - The kind that is meant to harm. It's not necessarily bad, but it often is.

*Deirfiúr* - Sisters in Irish.

Demons - Often employed to do evil. They live in various hells but can be released upon the earth if you know how to get to them and then get them out. If they are killed on Earth, they are sent back to their hell.

Dragon Sense - A FireSoul's ability to find treasure. It is an internal sense that pulls them toward what they seek. It is easiest to find gold, but they can find anything or anyone that is valued by someone.

Elemental Mage – A rare type of mage who can manipulate all of the elements.

Enchanted Artifacts – Artifacts can be imbued with magic that lasts after the death of the person who put the magic into the artifact (unlike a spell that has not been put into an artifact—these spells disappear after the Magica's death). But magic is not stable. After a period of time—hundreds or thousands of years depending on the circumstance—the magic will degrade. Eventually, it can go bad and cause many problems.

Fire Mage – A mage who can control fire.

FireSoul - A very rare type of Magica who shares a piece of the dragon's soul. They can locate treasure and steal the gifts (powers) of other supernaturals. With practice, they can manipulate the gifts they steal, becoming the strongest of that gift. They are despised and feared. If they are caught, they are thrown in the Prison of Magical Deviants.

The Great Peace - The most powerful piece of magic ever created. It hides magic from the eyes of humans.

Hearth Witch – A Magica who is versed in magic relating to hearth and home. They are often good at potions and protective spells and are also very perceptive when on their own turf.

Informa - A supernatural who can steal powers.

Magica - Any supernatural who has the power to create magic —witches, sorcerers, mages. All are governed by the Order of the Magica.

The Origin - The descendent of the original alpha shifter. They are the most powerful shifter and can turn into any species.

Order of the Magica - There are two governments that enforce law for supernaturals—the Alpha Council and the Order of the Magica. The Order of the Magica govern all Magica. They work cooperatively with the Alpha Council when necessary—for example, when capturing FireSouls.

Phantom - A type of supernatural that is similar to a ghost. They are incorporeal. They feed off the misery and pain of others, forcing them to relive their greatest nightmares and fears. They do not have a fully functioning mind like a human or supernatural. Rather, they are a shadow of their former selves. Half-bloods are extraordinarily rare.

Seeker - A type of supernatural who can find things. FireSouls often pass off their dragon sense as Seeker power.

Shifter - A supernatural who can turn into an animal. All are governed by the Alpha Council.

Transporter - A type of supernatural who can travel anywhere. Their power is limited and must regenerate after each use.

Vampire - Blood drinking supernaturals with great strength and speed who live in a separate realm.

Warden of the Underworld - A one of a kind position created by Roarke. He keeps order in the Underworld.

# ABOUT LINSEY

Before becoming a writer, Linsey Hall was a nautical archaeologist who studied shipwrecks from Hawaii and the Yukon to the UK and the Mediterranean. She credits fantasy and historical romances with her love of history and her career as an archaeologist. After a decade of tromping around the globe in search of old bits of stuff that people left lying about, she settled down and started penning her own romance novels. Her Dragon's Gift series draws upon her love of history and the paranormal elements that she can't help but include.

# COPYRIGHT

Copyright 2017 by Linsey Hall
Published by Bonnie Doon Press LLC

Linsey@LinseyHall.com
www.LinseyHall.com
https://www.facebook.com/LinseyHallAuthor
ISBN 978-1-942085-38-6